BRIGHT LIGHTS
AND PROMISES

Monique Dionne

iUniverse, Inc.
Bloomington

BRIGHT LIGHTS AND PROMISES

iUniverse books may be ordered through booksellers or by contacting:

iUniverse
1663 Liberty Drive
Bloomington, IN 47403
www.iuniverse.com
1-800-Authors (1-800-288-4677)

ISBN: 978-1-4759-8900-7 (sc)
ISBN: 978-1-4759-8901-4 (hc)
ISBN: 978-1-4759-8902-1 (e)

Library of Congress Control Number: 2013907963

Printed in the United States of America.

iUniverse rev. date: 5/7/2013

BRIGHT LIGHTS AND PROMISES

I could never have imagined how challenging or exhilarating and exhausting it would be to complete this project, however I fear I have freed a monster who can't wait to get started on the next one!

I would simply like to dedicate the birthing of my first book to my father who always inspired me to pursue my passion and everything else would take care of itself. Since he passed last October after a losing battle with pancreatic cancer, he whispered to me to complete my book.

My wonderful husband and friend as well as my three beautiful angels also supported this project with me, though often it abducted me from family time. They will be so proud of me when it is finally in hand.

Bright Lights and Promises

Monique Dionne

Bright Lights and Promises, is the first of many novels to be written by Monique and this particular novel was based on a decade of life experience and interesting individuals that work inside the walls of strip clubs around the country. Furthermore, though this lifestyle attracts a varying plethora of personalities, the young lady, Candy or Diana, is loosely based on a type of dancer that Monique encountered during her travels across the country.

Monique first began her journey in Detroit, next she popped up in Chicago, she also worked in Atlanta with a friend during the '96 Olympics, and then Tampa was next on her list. Later, Monique checked out Los Angeles and finally Las Vegas before making back home to Lansing, MI. Ultimately Monique has had varied an extensive experience in the adult entertainment industry, which will continue to have relevance in her remaining books, since she has literally dozens of stories to pull from. Mrs. Dionne has since turned her life over to motherhood and teaching Sunday school to young adults.

It is the hope of Monique, to one day to traverse the country and speak with many of the young ladies who, for various reasons, may find themselves trapped in that lifestyle and are searching for a way out of the industry. There is a huge preponderance of alcohol and drug abuse associated with that work and many of the ladies were simply not as lucky as Monique to have an education and a strong, supportive family structure to help them transition away from that work.

Chapter 1

Now that is one hot lady, Crispin thought. He'd seen her before, but had managed to avoid her sensual persuasions. However tonight, he felt inexplicably drawn towards her. She had white blonde hair and was hanging upside down from a twenty-foot tall brass pole, secured only by her ankles, which tightly gripped the pole for security. He could tell why this dancer was called Candy; a man could get a cavity just watching her. She had naughty written all over her, but it was obvious to him that she was sophisticated as well. *It's clear that I need to possess this woman*, he mused. She seemed so wild and free, so independent, sultry, and unrestrained as she laughed and beamed down at all the guys staring up at her. As the drunken men whistled and jeered at her, throwing dollar bills and more from the tip bar, she gladly strolled around the stage, collecting her tips.

Crispin, a Nephilim, (Hebrew for a fallen angel-human hybrid), was conflicted with his humanity while watching her. His father, who had also been a Nephilim, had explained to him when he was a youth of twelve that there was no way for him to get into heaven after being dismissed or fallen because now he was simply a demon in human form. Much like Lucifer himself, Crispin had become sin due to his paternity.

However, having lived in Las Vegas for the past ten years and securing a well-paid salary as a financial consultant with a rapidly growing finance company, he'd managed to keep his dark secret under wraps. He lived a rather secluded and lonely lifestyle but occasionally indulged in various evil, self-fulfilling acts whenever he deemed necessary. While he had become relatively successful, he attempted to avoid emotional involvements altogether except for a few friends from his workplace and a couple of Nephilim friends, who occasionally asked him out for a few beers. But because he was still a man, he sometimes engaged in an escort to quell his carnal desires; escorts were not terribly difficult to find in Las Vegas.

Now Crispin had eyes on Candy, and it was obvious to him that this exotic dancer was very sexy and extremely at ease in this loud, smoky environment; he'd seen many dancers before her, but she was definitely different, she didn't let the drama around her to affect her in the least. *I have to have her*, he thought. *I know if I can just get her in my presence for a few minutes, I could persuade and seduce this sexy exotic woman.*

After she exited the stage, Crispin watched her work for about an hour. She moved swiftly, confidently, and with sexy sophistication; she was clearly a pro. Very few customers dared turn her down for a couch dance, which cost them about twenty-five dollars each. After lengthy and careful deliberation, Crispin skillfully and smoothly sat down in her line of fire so she would be forced to ask him for a dance.

Part of him couldn't help but wonder if he should even pursue this carnal objective of his. He was so intensely attracted to her that his human nature might get the better of him and he might find it difficult to use her or manipulate her. He'd denied her before, but he would not tonight.

She was so different than the other girls, almost too intelligent and virtuous to be in a place like this. Crispin could sense her strong religious upbringing. *But I can change all that*, he thought. *I need to get to know her, even though I'm sure she gets asked out a dozen times a night. But not by me yet, and that's going to make all the difference, I'm certain.* He smiled nefariously to himself.

Crispin was beginning to think that it had been a while since he'd been laid, and watching Candy glide around the club in a hot red slinky fitted dress and red platform heels forced his mind in one direction. He knew it was far more enjoyable to allow his human male side to take over and indulge himself occasionally. Sure, like many of his business colleagues, he eyeballed good-looking girls all the time, but generally he felt forced to keep his distance. But not tonight. Now he found himself standing there in that club, daydreaming about Candy. Though he'd been abstaining from the couch dance scene, which he found ridiculously expensive and unfulfilling, he realized it may be the only time he'd get a chance to get close to her. Besides, it wasn't love; it was purely lust, he mused.

Candy wasn't an average exotic dancer. She was a business woman who had been raised in a devout Catholic family. Her mother had been a prominent paralegal in a top-ranking Vegas law firm, and her father was a high-powered, high-earning plastic surgeon to the stars (and proudly responsible for Candy's voluptuous 36DD breast augmentation). When she began college, she had never returned because their constant supervision was exhausting. She was an only child, so she had felt saddened to be leaving her mother alone in their big house, but she always had brunch with her folks on Sundays after church. They were good people and deserved to know what was going on in her life. They had given her just about anything her heart desired, and she had always been a good girl.

But once she was introduced to a career that permitted her to continue her lavish lifestyle while looking for a postgraduate job, she couldn't resist the temptation. She had grown up with money, and she was not going to be without it, even if it meant doing a less than reputable career. She managed to hide it from her folks for a year, before it occurred to her that implants would add a huge increase to her already lofty income. One day a customer came into the club and showed Diana a picture of Coco, the hot, blonde, busty wife of the famous rap star Ice-T. He explained to Diana that she would be almost an identical replica of Coco if she had her breasts done as well. She thought it was excellent idea to be a celebrity twin (It could only improve her revenue, and it had by almost double). Even though her parents were divorced, they had an amicable relationship with one another and shared a deep love of Diana, their only child. They also still shared the same residence, though they maintained separate bedrooms. Like with many couples, this living arrangement was financially prudent for both people and they agreed they would change their living arrangements if either of them decided to have another relationship that would require more privacy.

Diana, who hadn't really needed to dance, had found herself rather surreptitiously thrown into the shady, mysterious world of exotic dance because of a simple double-dare bet she'd made with a frenemy. In exotic dance, she had found a special calling and silent rebellion. Her friend had bet her that she would never do such a thing; however, Diana had won the bet. She had been ready to rebel. She needed no cajoling on amateur night, she was ready to go, after she'd had a few drinks to calm her nerves. She could finally break free from being daddy's little girl, she had thought. However, she had eventually had to explain her new job to her parents.

It turned out to be not nearly as awful as she had expected. She had told her father first; he'd been worldly and always seemed a bit more open-minded than her mom. Her mother was immediately wary and quickly became worried that Diana might end up dead. No doubt, there was a seedy stigma associated with strippers. But Cynthia's husband had reassured her and encouraged her to let their daughter live a bit and make some of her own decisions for a while, after all she was an adult he had reminded her; he trusted her as long as she always stayed in contact with them and finished her education so she could someday land a "real" job when maturity finally kicked in. Neither of them had expected it to last very long.

Candy had soon learned that keeping a boyfriend or meeting a respectable man while in this profession was simply impossible, and she often thought of quitting. Clearly, meeting a man with a mind for business, a respectable income at least comparable to her own, and great sex would be rather refreshing, especially after having gone out with so many losers who had turned out to be possessive and jealous of her high-stakes, high-paying, and sexually pervasive lifestyle in adult entertainment. She intended to keep her lifestyle for as long as her body and face would allow because, no doubt, *gravity sucked*. The truth was that love didn't pay the bills, at least not so far, besides she was only 25, what was the big hurry anyway? There's no prize in settling down too young. She had only been working this job for the past five years until she had saved enough to afford her sharp Humvee and put enough down on her condo, for her father to cosign.

As Crispin stood in the shadows of the fancy high-end nightclub, carefully watching Candy hustle customers for dances, her skin shining and glistening under the bright, hot multicolored stage lights, she looked over at him and tossed him a cavalier kiss and a quick wink. He couldn't help but also notice that her body was so lean and muscular yet still soft and feminine. Oh, if only he could control his feelings of carnal desire. But she was so long, tight, and incredibly shapely, with a pretty gold chain dangling around her waist, that his inner demon continued to urge him on. This lady exuded sexuality with every curve. The truth was that he really didn't want to control his attraction to her any longer; he'd already been cursed as a demon and was ready to get to work on his next victim. Or so he thought.

Crispin took pride in how well he kept himself. He was tall and handsome, dressed in an expensive, elegant blue pinstriped suit. Carefully watching, seldom sitting, and often swirling a short glass of vodka. His demon spirit made him restless, and he found it difficult to sit down for long periods of time. He enjoyed the simple fact that his height, though not an anomaly, intimidated the average guys standing around him. He was a classic fallen angel by all accounts. He knew that he was strangely beautiful, and he was looking forward to a couch dance from Candy.

Many of the dancers were naturally drawn to him. Much like the Pied Piper of Hamelin, he was magical and magnetic. They enjoyed the challenge of his denial. However, tonight he had eyes only for Candy and casually dismissed the others with total disregard. Finally, she arrived at where he'd briefly sat down. She smiled and licked her lips while staring into his bright green eyes and slowly caressed his hand and thigh. Bending over him carefully to expose her cleavage, she nuzzled his neck and with a soft, hot breath whispered in his ear, asking him to go upstairs with her to the VIP room for a more private, intimate dance.

Crispin was delighted and supposed she was one of the highest earners at the club because her simple physical approach and contact was extremely arousing, persuasive, and unlike any approach he'd experienced that night. He surprised himself that he'd never had a dance by her before. It occurred to him that the customers who turned her down probably knew she was expensive and therefore felt she was out of their league. Just as Candy was pulling Crispin upstairs toward the club's VIP lounge, he bumped into another Nephilim coming down with another dancer. As they passed, they nodded silently in acknowledgment, as one demon clearly recognized another.

Once in the room, Candy motioned to Crispin to sit in a big, black, comfortable leather chair, one approximately a dozen chairs in the VIP lounge. Then she proceeded to strut sexily over to the jukebox, upon which the ladies took turns playing their favorite songs to couch dance to.

When she returned to him and slid into his lap, she said, "Wow. You are the tallest and hottest guy I've danced for all night. But you probably get that all the time, right? You're probably going to tell me you're a professional ball player or something. Anyway, I believe I'm going to enjoy this dance myself." Candy straightened her dress and then cuddled herself into Crispin's lap awaiting her chosen song to begin on the jukebox.

"Well, not really, but thanks," Crispin said, making an effort to appear shy, yet enjoying the warmth of Candy's body next to his. "I've seen you before, but I've never given in to the couch dance idea, I always felt they were over-rated and overpriced. Perhaps you can change my mind. Candy smiled and nodded as if she were certain she could. "I work quite a bit. I have a home office which allows me to not always have to go into the office. It's great because I can make my own hours. I'm a financial consultant actually, not a ball player. Sorry. Not so exciting, huh? But I figured if I'm going to finally come up here, I wanted it to be with you, since you are clearly the sexiest dancer in this club." He flashed his porcelain white teeth at her as he grinned.

Candy tried hard to compose herself again, not wanting Crispin to see her flustered by his presence. "Thanks" she replied. "I'll do my best so just sit back, relax, and let me do my thing. Maybe I can take your mind off work for a few minutes or so."

Right then her song began to play on the jukebox. It was one of her favorite slow jams by Bruno Mars: "It Will Rain." She automatically went into character. She began by running her fingers through his hair. As she stared deeply into his gorgeous green eyes, she felt an erotic sensation, a tingly spark she had never felt before when doing a couch dance. It was almost as if he was giving off some strange, warm energy. *Damn, this guy is so fucking hot.* Next, she slid her dress up her thighs and very slowly straddled Crispin in a seductive pose. Then in an almost gymnast like move, she put her leg on his shoulder, her thigh brushing his nose and ear. Crispin turned to sniff her perfume and skin; it was intoxicating. During the entire dance, she never stopped moving seductively to the music and staring deeply into his eyes. She was certain to always maintain contact with him throughout her dance, heightening its intimacy. It was apparent to her that she was just as excited to be dancing for him as he was. Under his hypnotic stare, she could feel her thong become moist with excitement. She attempted to reign in her impulses unsuccessfully. She was suddenly overcome by his erotic spirit and found herself kissing him on his lips. She had never been so brazen before, but she couldn't contain herself. She felt inexplicably drawn to him.

Crispin did not back away, as this was part of his seductive plan, but he automatically clutched her ass to keep her from falling off his lap as she moved to the music. She couldn't control herself and threw herself completely into the song and the dance. All she could think about was wrapping her legs around him in bed. This show of emotion certainly violated all the rules of the couch dance. Thankfully, it was relatively dark in the VIP lounge. The other girls didn't notice nor seem to care about Candy's sudden reckless display of emotion. Tony, the bouncer on duty, just grinned at her and shook his head naughtily. He knew Candy always shared the wealth at the end of the night when tip-out time came around.

Next she did a full-on lap grind that simulated a dry fuck to the beat of the music, and this only escalated the arousal between them. No doubt the fireworks between them had begun.

Wow. This is pretty cool. No wonder so many fellows come up here. It sucks that it has to end like this, though; I think I'm going to need a finale, Crispin thought, wanting to grab her ass again but abstaining to avoid breaking the no-touch rule again. But Candy seemed to hear his thoughts.

"You've never been up here before, huh? I don't do this type of dance for all my customers. We're supposed to maintain at least a six-inch distance from the customer, during the dance. I would totally get fired if my manager saw me breaking the rules. But I'm going to make sure you come back up here with me again, it's so worth it. I think I might just want you all to myself. But sorry, there are no finales in the VIP room." She faced him again as the song wound down. Candy quickly stood up and began to pull her costume back on, before collapsing in Crispin's lap again, breathless but awaiting the next song to dance to. Crispin thoroughly enjoyed the closeness of Candy's body next to his own. As well of the fact that she had no problem making eye contact with him, which he found difficult for most women.

She grabbed one of her breasts, while chatting with him and, brought the nipple to her mouth, and began to flick it with her tongue as close to his face as possible without touching his nose. Candy was mesmerized by his stare, which simply fixated her; he wasn't like other guys she had danced for. Crispin was turned on by her boldness. He tried to adjust himself, but couldn't conceal his erection.

"You know, you're so hot, I'd be willing to dance for you again on the house if that's okay with you," Candy teased him, and he was all in. Actually, it was no big deal for her to give away a free dance occasionally, since she always met her financial goal for the evening. Besides, since she was equally aroused dancing for this tall, mysterious, beautiful customer, it wasn't going to be a problem for her. Trying to control her enthusiasm, on the other hand, would.

"What's your name, anyway," she asked him, smiling, trying to contain her arousal and keep a poker face. It would be even better to personalize him at this point, deleting him from her mental "just another customer" file.

"My name is Crispin," he answered her with a straight face, his eyes fixated on her breasts as she began to undress again. "I've already decided that I'd like to take you out to dinner and show you a good time. I'm sure you're going to say no, but"—he knew she was already under his spell—"it's worth asking anyway."

Candy looked him deeply in the eyes and said sheepishly, "Well, I don't generally go out with customers, but I could probably make an exception for you."

Crispin smiled, and they proceeded to save each other's numbers in their cell phones.

"You haven't told me your name yet," he queried, grinning devilishly at her.

"Oh, my bad. My real name is Diana. Please forgive me. Candy is my stage name, but I urge you to check out my website. I'll give you a business card with my website address on it."

After spending two hundred dollars in couch dances on Candy, primarily to keep her to himself for a while, he couldn't wait to get back to his luxurious home, which was sporadically littered with Bibles and research books, historical pictures, and notebooks he was using to try to uncover the dark secrets of his past. He thought it might be a good idea to be well read and knowledgeable just in case he may have to someday explain himself to someone he deemed important enough to care about, something he desperately wanted, though he wrestled with the idea of a relationship; however, he was still angry with God for taking his mother. He shared his place with no one, so his secret was carefully safeguarded from visitors.

He quickly ran to his home office and pulled up Candy's website to satisfy his curiosity and learn more about her. Crispin was delighted that she'd given him her real home and cell number so she could go out on a date with him. He was excited to see that her website had been beautifully and professionally created, with hundreds of her own pictures, videos and intellectual commentary of her past college life, her ordinary life, and her updated touring schedule; it even featured a pay-per-view asset for visitors to enjoy her dancing videos. He was slightly tortured by the fact that he was smitten by her effervescent spirit and good looks, as he perused her photos and videos.

He became even more aroused until he ultimately masturbated to climax. He was conflicted that it was a great feeling of release, but he couldn't help but considering what God would think of this minor infraction. Crispin became angry again because he didn't like to feel shameful, always concerning himself with the wrath of God. It was far more fulfilling to give in to his hedonistic desires and deny the existence and judgment of a superior being.

His thoughts were interrupted by Candy's fabulous website. Luckily for him, there was also a message board where customers could leave colorful comments. He was compelled to leave her a message. He typed a short comment: Those were the most fabulous dances I've ever had. I can't wait for dinner. *She must be making a pretty decent income to afford such a fancy website with videos of her dancing all over the country.* In the pictures and videos, she was doing various pole tricks and winning all sorts of competitions and such. Of course, her twenty-five-year-old body was a personal trainer's dream and clearly built for speed and stamina.

While staring her, her face made Crispin recall images of his mother, another beautiful human woman, whom his father had met working in one of the many casinos in town. He had never had an opportunity to meet her because of her untimely death during his birth. He missed knowing her greatly. Ultimately, Crispin was raised by his father. Because Nephilim were the offspring of a male fallen angel and a female human, were often referred to as giants in the Hebrew Bible, and many had apparently been washed away by the Great Flood, many Christians doubted their very existence. They were only spoken about briefly in the book of Genesis, before the flood, and they were never discussed in this way, by most Christian theologians. Most people were completely unaware of their legendary and mythical existence.

Crispin could understand his carnal attraction to Candy, whom he'd been watching and surveying for some time now. Crispin generally managed to avoid the club scene where Candy worked for fear of his intense human attraction to her, but recently he had been finding it harder and harder to do; she had an extremely powerful allure, much like him. However, since Crispin was half angel, he still retained a fair amount of supernatural power handed down to him via his father, he knew it would be far too easy to seduce her and probably unfair, but he had never really concerned himself with being fair.

Crispin enjoyed using his devious ways to manipulate and control situations in his favor, whether it was money, love, or sex, though love he tried to avoid; human emotions were far too complicated, even for him. His primary concern with Candy, however, was whether or not he really needed to manipulate her. She seemed to already show great interest in him. Maybe he didn't need to push her much. What if she just liked him enough as a regular guy and he didn't have to work at seducing her? That would be even better. Crispin was eagerly looking forward to the next time they met.

Chapter 2

Ding-dong, ding-dong, the doorbell rang. Somebody would not stop ringing the damn doorbell. Jessie, another dancer at Olympia Gardens and a close friend to Diana, stormed down the long hallway of the condo she and Diana shared. It was her boyfriend, Chad, with his standard quarter-inch facial hair, drenched in Armani cologne, and draped in his typical black silk shirt. He had a preoccupation with strippers, so Jessie (who went by the stage name Lexus) was not his first and would not be his last.

"Oh my God, Chad, what the hell are you doing here so early?" Jessica yawned, wiping the sleep from her eyes and attempting to look angry, but she really wasn't because he was so easy on the eye.

"Early?" Chad answered, already aroused and ready to get freaky with his half-naked girlfriend.

It was not unusual for the girls to sleep in until noon after getting in from the club around five thirty in the morning. Stroking his already anxious erection through his slacks, he quickly pulled her into his arms and gave her a huge bear hug.

Smiling, he said, "It's almost lunchtime, baby, but I think I've got a better idea before we go to lunch!" With that, he quickly swiped her up off her feet and disappeared into her bedroom, laughing.

Ding-dong, the doorbell rang again; Diana sighed. Now that Jessica was all tied up, it was her turn to get the door. This morning was already turning into a nightmare of no more sleep. Since Jessie was unavailable,

Diana dragged herself from her warm bed and down comforter, grabbed her robe from the door hook, and rubbed her eyes. She bumped into Chad on the way to the front door.

"Sorry, Chad. I kinda didn't see you," she mumbled.

However, Chad had clearly seen her, as he always did whenever he dropped by. He always kept a keen eye on his girlfriends' roommates.

Diana went to the door and opened it. It was someone serving her a bench warrant from an old speeding ticket she'd been ignoring. After signing for the warrant, Diana headed back to her bedroom, where her cat, Freckles, lay coiled at the end of her Tempurpedic bed. Chad and Jessica were already going at it in the bedroom next door. It never took Jessie long to get in the mood when Chad showed up. There was loud giggling and low moans emanating from her bedroom, so Diana rolled her eyes and closed the door to her bedroom.

Of course, Chad was nothing short of a Greek sex god. He had the typical middle-Eastern characteristics; beautiful olive-toned skin, about five foot ten, his hair was black, mid-length, and wavy. He had dark, sultry eyes and a lean athletic frame. But he was so full of himself that he enjoyed parading around their condo shirtless, proudly revealing a knife wound he'd suffered from a bar fight over his last stripper girlfriend, who'd had a crazy ex-boyfriend. He thought the scar made him look tough. He was awash in arrogance.

Diana knew he couldn't be trusted as far as Jessie could throw him, and she regularly warned her friend of this. Jessie knew it, but she enjoyed gloating to the other dancers about her incredibly hot, rich boyfriend from Lebanon whose father was in the oil business and always eager to send money to his spoiled son in America. It was all about the great sex and the cocaine he always supplied her with, and everybody knew it.

Candy had never gotten into the drug scene, so she couldn't understand why her friend worked so hard all night only to blow half of it on coke. Clearly there were more material things she could do with the money, like designer bags, shoes, new costumes, and such. Better yet, she could actually try paying her bills on time. But as long as Jessie had Chad to help her out in a pinch. Diana didn't let it get to her.

Her loss, Diana figured. It's not like they could dance forever and make this kind of easy money. Jessie would probably just end up broke and strung out like a bunch of other ex-dancers because there was no way Chad was going to hang around a cokehead dancer for long. Hopefully she'd be able to keep up her end of the rent when Chad was gone, which was inevitable. But at least she wasn't begging Diana for money. *So whatever*, Diana figured. Jessie had turned out to be a really good friend to Diana and always provided a shoulder to cry on when needed. Trying not to be judgmental, she rolled over and tried to get back to sleep, Diana had been taught by her father that she could only control her own actions and not others.

Fifteen minutes later, her phone buzzed. Diana reached over to her night table and grabbed her cell phone, already agitated that her restful sleep had been disturbed. "Yeah, hello?" she answered in an especially groggy and irritated tone.

"Hello, Diana. Sorry to wake you. This is Sister Lori Peters from your mother's church. I promised her that I'd check in on you this week. Cynthia's a good friend to me."

Diana immediately let out a groan. *Ugh*, no wonder she hadn't recognized the number on her caller ID.

"Yeah, so what can I do for you today?" Diana asked sarcastically.

She was very much aware of how much her mother detested and worried about her new occupation. Her mother had been trying for some time to coerce her to go back to church, so far to no avail. But since Diana loved and respected her mother so deeply, she always obliged her when the dreaded church ladies called. She had been raised a devout Catholic for her parents' sake, but she had always craved the bad girl lifestyle. She once saw a bumper sticker that read, *Good girls go to heaven, but bad girls go everywhere! She knew right away that she wanted to be a bad girl for a while.*

"You know, Sister Peters, I know my mother gave you my number so you can come over and give me a Bible study or whatever and try to talk me back into joining the church, but I should warn you that I'm really not that interested in another Bible study right now. I happen to love my job, even though I have a degree in business management. I know

I can't do this forever. It's fun, exciting, and flexible, and the money is really good," she said, wondering why she was explaining herself to this Miss Goody Two-Shoes.

"Well, I understand, dear. How about I just swing by to introduce myself so we won't be strangers anymore?" the nun gently pleaded.

"Um, not today, ma'am." Diana thought it seemed like a sneaky little way of coming by to check on her. "However, that would be fine for twenty minutes or so maybe this weekend. Like Saturday, late morning or something. Not too early because I generally sleep in late." *Anything to make this lady stop calling is great with me already. God, why does my mother keep doing this to me? Hasn't she figured out that I'm a grown woman now and I don't need her permission to live my life?*

"I'm sorry, Sister Peters. I'm still a bit groggy from work last night. Did you need me to give you directions?"

"Sure, if it's not too much trouble, dear," she replied, even more syrupy than before.

"Well, do you know where Yorkshire Terrace Condominiums are, on the edge of town? We live at 2825, the building straight to the back, overlooking the pond. It's pretty easy, actually. Just ring the bell, condo 245, and Jessie, my roommate, or I will let you in. So when were you planning on dropping by?"

Diana hoped Sister Lori would say she wasn't free until next week, next year, or better yet, never. However, Diana knew there was no way to get out of this appointment with Sis. Lori, regardless of how hard she might try.

"Actually, I have a dentist appointment tomorrow, and I'm sure the church book club meets at my house Thursday afternoon," Sister Lori replied sadly. "I'll just try you later on near the weekend and see when we can get together. Okay?" she whispered softly.

Yes, great, now I can delay her until Saturday, at least. Diana thought. *I'll be sure to save this number under Lori Church Lady so I can ignore it the next time she calls.* Why couldn't her mom be more like her dad when it came to her life and be more laid back, still concerned but not neurotic? Well, since her father had been raised in the rough boroughs of New York—Manhattan, more precisely—he was a bit more jaded than her mom. There was very little her dad hadn't seen or done in his youth, so his shock threshold was pretty high. Clearly that explained quite a bit.

An hour later, when Diana finally made her way out of her soft, warm down comforter, she noticed a bruise forming on her leg from a new pole trick she had done in the club last night. *Oh well, I'll just use some cover-up later*, she thought. She hurried into her sports bra, sweats, and gym shoes and rushed out the door to get to the gym, where she was supposed to meet her trainer, Jackie. She tossed her duffel bag into the backseat of her bright red Hummer, which she'd bought off a customer for a real sweet deal, and charged out of her private condo neighborhood.

Oops. She realized she'd forgotten to holler at Jessie and mention where she was headed, but Jessie was probably too preoccupied with Chad at the time to care. Diana noticed on her way out of her condominiums that they were beginning to build a new play area for the kids of all the new families moving in. *Someday that would be her*, she thought to herself as she smiled driving out.

Chapter 3

"Oh my God, Jackie, I'm so sorry I'm late today!" Diana yelled over to Jackie, who waved but was working with another client still. Diana headed to the locker room straightaway to finish dressing.

"Hey, girl. I didn't know you worked out here too!"

Diana swerved around to see who the unfamiliar voice had come from. It belonged to another dancer called Layla. Diana secretly rolled her eyes; the last thing she wanted right now was to see another dancer from work on her off time. But since it was protocol for a dancer not to refer to another dancer by her stage name in public, Diana was at a loss for words, briefly, but not for a big smile.

"Yeah, hey, I do. But what's your real name? I don't think we've ever met before. Aren't you a day-shift girl?" Diana recalled seeing her briefly during a shift change.

"Yeah, I do, and actually my real name is Layla too. But I can see you're in a hurry, and I still need to flatiron my hair, so take care," she replied, wiping her freckled face with a club towel. Her curly red hair was beginning to frizz from the pool humidity seeping into the girls' locker room from the pool area.

They both smiled at each other again. Happy to be free from conversation with Layla, Diana slammed her locker shut and spun the combo on the lock. She called, "See ya! Gotta get with my trainer," and headed back out to the gym, where Jackie was now waiting for her.

Jackie was the most sought after trainer at 24/7 Fitness. Diana had signed with her the first day she was allowed on the floor. She had been certain by the looks of Jackie's body that she was highly qualified, and so far Diana had been right. Besides, Jackie didn't really care what Diana did for a living as long as she was able to pay her $100 per hour fee. Diana felt proud that she was one of the first fifty clients Jackie trained throughout the week. While Diana was already in great shape from dancing more than five years, Jackie enjoyed taking personal credit for how good she looked. The truth was that Jackie had been delighted when Diana asked if she could put a link to Jackie's website on her own website. This way both ladies would win. Jackie had already received five referrals from Diana's site.

Chapter 4

After Diana completed training with Jackie, she figured she had enough time to drop by the mall to grab lunch and get her nails filled. Much to her surprise, Layla's bright yellow and black Nike athletic bag was still in the locker room, and Layla was in the farthest bathroom stall, sniveling and weeping to herself.

Diana quietly approached the stall, whispering, "Layla? Layla, is that you?" She gently pushed the partially closed stall door and saw Layla sitting on a toilet seat, fully clothed, her hair only halfway flat ironed, and her knees pulled up to her wet, splotchy face.

"Oh my God, are you okay, Layla? What happened since I last saw you?"

Layla just looked up at her, dazed, and shook her head, unconvinced. "Why do you care? You're only the most popular dancer at the club. Even I know that much…"

Diana could see this wasn't going to be easy, but since they were the only two ladies in the locker room at the moment, she proceeded, attempting to fake concern.

"I don't think that has anything to do with why you're so upset, right? I can see your flatiron is still out and on over there. I'm sure that's not what's got you down. I hope." She smiled weakly at Layla.

"No, it doesn't, Candy," Layla said her stage name in a sneering, taunting voice while smearing her tears across her face with the back of her hand. At this point Layla just seemed irritated by her concern, so

Diana figured she should just move on with her day and forget about Layla and her troubles, which obviously didn't involve her anyhow.

"You know, I was just trying to help, but if you're gonna be all bitchy about it, just forget it!" Diana quickly snatched up her bag and stormed toward the locker room door, leaving Layla to cry alone in the stall.

"Wait! Thanks!" Layla finally called out. "I was raped yesterday after work by my boyfriend."

"Oh shit." Diana spun back around to face Layla, who was now standing outside the stall, leaning against the wall, and looking pretty pathetic. *I really don't want to get involved*, Diana mused glumly. *I barely know this chick.* Well, it was too late now, and she was the only one standing there facing Layla. She felt obligated to do or say something. "Wow, Layla. That's really fucked up! I'm so sorry. I hope you called the police. But I don't really know you or your boyfriend that well, so I feel a little weird getting involved."

Diana then dropped her bag and began to walk slowly toward Layla, who was trembling and tearing up again. Then Layla fell into Diana's arms and began to cry loudly. It was not the kind of scene someone would typically want to make public. Surprised at the suddenness of it all, Diana gently pulled the distressed girl into the small sitting area outside the dressing room. They sat next to one another on a sofa.

Suddenly, Jackie appeared in the doorway and extended her hand toward Layla. "Come on, honey. Let's go to my office for a bit. I overheard you."

Layla immediately stood and, in a trance, took Jackie's hand and stared cautiously into her eyes. They walked out of the little room together after Layla turned to hug and thank Diana. Jackie motioned to Diana to get going because she had everything under control.

Wow! That was weird! Diana thought. This was not the way she had expected her morning to go, but being the flexible person she was, she could only presume that Layla would be all right by the way she seemed comforted by Jackie. *Hopefully I don't have any more glitches in my schedule today, maybe I can finally get back to my initial schedule for today before I go to work,* Diana thought as she tossed her bag over her shoulder and headed out of the gym. As it were, she may have spoken too soon about her day.

As Diana headed toward her Humvee, she saw Crispin sitting outside in his silver Corvette convertible.

"Well hello, stranger. What are you doing over here?" She couldn't hide her surprise or the big bright smile on her face. "You remembered where I told you I worked out?" Neither could she help her natural suspicion of a customer showing up at the place she worked out, especially this one. At first it seemed a bit creepy to her; however, the flood of excitement from the memory of their recent couch dance quickly clouded her judgment. *Hopefully he's not some queer stalker guy,* she thought, giggling to herself and feeling a bit self-conscious about her looks.

"Actually, yeah, I did. I thought maybe we could go for lunch if you're not too busy. I don't want to interrupt your workout or anything. I could only hope you were still here, because I called your house first, and your roommate said you'd gone to the gym."

His smile was dazzling, but again Diana felt trepid. *Oh, what the hell*, she thought. *Lunch would be a nice distraction.* "Sounds great. My whole morning has been a bit different today; but I'm all done training, but I'm a mess. I'm sorry. I didn't expect such a hot lunch date to show up! So are you driving or am I?" she asked.

Crispin climbed out of his car, wearing a polo shirt and jeans from work, walked around to the passenger side, and opened the door for her to hop in. "Does this answer your question?" he asked, motioning to the passenger seat like a flight attendant.

"Hmm, so chivalry is not dead. I wish I was dressed a little better." She giggled as she climbed into his car. "But you'll need to bring me back to get my ride, okay?"

"Don't worry. You look fine. Besides, it's a surprise visit. What would I expect you to be dressed like? Certainly not the clothes you work in, silly" Crispin flashed his Hollywood smile, and his green eyes beckoned her.

Diana couldn't resist his spell, and she didn't want to.

"And sure. It's no problem. I'll be happy to bring you back; I'm glad you're joining me for lunch instead of presuming I'm a serial killer." He chuckled at her, happy to have at least gained some of her trust.

Diana quickly called Jackie back in the gym to let her know she was leaving her vehicle for a little while. *Hmm, I think I could get used to this guy*, she thought.

They decided to eat at one of the local hotel casinos because they wanted to eat quickly while Crispin was on his lunch hour. As they raced down the Vegas Strip, Crispin reached over and laid his hand on Candy's exposed leg, grinning salaciously at her as he rubbed her smooth leg.

"You are unusually soft for someone who appears so muscular," he said.

She welcomed his touch and slowly relaxed her thighs.

"I'm delighted you decided to come to lunch with me," he said.

"Yeah, me too, but I wish you would've let me go home and shower and change first." Candy giggled. She was still in her spandex workout shorts and well-worn sweatshirt with her sports bra peeking out.

Crispin just shook his head and smiled. "No, no time for all of that Di, besides that wouldn't be such a surprise, then. All through lunch Crispin couldn't take his eyes off her as he attempted to trap her in his seductive trance. He knew that the next time they met up—and he knew there would be a next time—he would go in for the kill. The kill of his skill, of course.

"I really enjoyed your dance last night. The fact that I got an extra special dance made it all the more enticing, you know. I have gone to the VIP room before, however I came away thinking that it was a terrible waste of time and money. The dancer spent like five minutes with me, but all she really wanted was more dances and more money. Clearly, I didn't feel like that with you at all, you're pretty special. I've been distracted all day thinking about it and hoping that I get a more personal one later on." Crispin winked at her to see if his seduction was working.

"Of course you can. I enjoyed giving you those dances. I'm not generally that easy, but I'd be thrilled to give you a personal dance after a real planned date, like dinner and a show." She could barely contain her delight at the thought of another date with Crispin. He was insanely hot, she thought, but probably unavailable, which made her feel more undesirable since today she was not the same glamorous girl he'd met at the club the previous night.

After they finished lunch (Diana wasn't the type of girl who was too shy to eat in front of a guy), they hurried out of the casino. Crispin had the valet pull up his car and opened Candy's door. Then he hopped into the driver's seat and took her back to the gym to retrieve her vehicle. His demon spirit was on full gentleman alert, patiently waiting to make his move as he rushed around to get her door again once they arrived. Then like a bolt of lightning he was at her Humvee, getting her door and giving her a long passionate kiss good-bye. His hands glided slowly down her thighs.

"Until next time, sugar," he said as he winked at her and sped off to work in his Corvette.

No doubt, he is a charmer, she thought. However, she'd already learned that if it looked too good to be true, it probably was. She figured his sudden interest in her was to get laid as soon as possible, but it was her style to allow things to progress smoothly and not give in too soon. She clearly wasn't a prude, but she wanted to savor his flavor first and feel him out a bit more.

Chapter 5

As Candy finally pulled into a parking space at Olympia Garden (which was wide enough for her new bright red Humvee), she already felt fatigued by the day's surprises. First there had been Chad's pop-up visit to see Jessie; next she had gotten served the bench warrant; then there had been the church lady and Layla's shocking locker-room confession at the gym about her boyfriend. However, the highlight had been the surprise lunch visit by the way-too-handsome Crispin.

But Candy knew there was something about getting onstage in costume and stripping in front of all of those eager, hungry eyes that would make her forget about the stupid anxieties of the day. She could always depend on the cheering crowd and the tips hitting the stage after her performance to blur the often meaningless, monotonous days. There was nothing like a few hundred dollar bills to change the course of her thoughts.

Since it was later in the week, the club was already busy with customers rolling in after work and hanging out for several hours with clients, attempting to close deals before the weekend over a few beers and a fancy chef's burger. Immediately the thought that if she worked hard, she could probably make it a thousand-dollar night put her in a good mood. If not a thousand, maybe seven-fifty; but at this point in her career she didn't really concern herself too much over a nights' earnings since she had already saved an ample amount of money, unlike her roommate and most other dancers, but being a college grad, certainly gave her an advantage over the other girls in the business.

She sat in her truck for few moments to contemplate if she really even wanted to go in tonight. This was the constant emotional conundrum of every dancer, whether to walk away from a socially unacceptable job making obscene amounts of cash in a very short time or to be a waitress on her feet all day collecting paltry tips and but have an acceptable reputation. Many of her friends had graduated as well, but were still sleeping on their parents' sofa waiting for the phone to ring with their dream job on the other end. Meanwhile she had a cool ride a posh pad and money to burn on whatever excesses she desired. Yet, the vision of a family with a cute house and picket fence still floated through her mind occasionally. She couldn't wait for the day when she could walk out and finally call it quits. Unfortunately that would not be today; she had a handsome mortgage now and a hefty car note. Maybe something or someone who could break the seduction of this job as well as keep her financially secure would come along; after all, she did have her college degree to consider, though she was fully aware that dancing would be the easiest money she ever made. After pondering her life, outside the club for fifteen minutes, she decided she should force herself to go in.

She always went into work with a financial goal and made sure to check her purse throughout the night to stay focused. Other girls spent countless wasted hours drinking through their shifts and getting high, basically not working hard enough to make more than a measly two hundred and fifty dollars the entire shift because work for them was really just social time. Not so, for Candy, time was money in her eyes and if she was going to be there, she damn sure was going to give it her all.

Chapter 6

It was not uncommon for Candy and some of the other top dancers to hang out with their "regulars" on the couches for a while, but they were still being paid to engage in the sometimes meaningless conversations (conversations most gentlemen would feel uncomfortable having with their wives, particularly sexual topics). Strippers were the perfect easy-listening counselors for the average guy because they were in a position of nonjudgment, whether the guy was an accountant or an auto mechanic or whether he wanted to discuss his gay son or daughter or why his wife no longer gave him blow jobs.

Oh what drama, Candy thought as she waved at the bartender and headed downstairs to the dancers' dressing room. The dressing room was already cloudy with hairspray and men's cologne (many dancers wore cologne to help disguise where their customers had been when they returned home to their wives). Candy didn't wear men's cologne, since living in Vegas meant having access to the best and most expensive perfumes on the market. The dressing room was also full of excessive chatting and gossiping between the girls.

"Hey, Miss Candy Apples!" one of the girls turned and yelled at her. "I hope you're gonna leave a little money for us tonight!" They jeered at her.

"Maybe if you're lucky I might!" Candy teased back. She was well aware that though the other girl's loved her for her gorgeous looks, her dry humor, and her bodacious breasts, they still took her for a serious threat. It made it all the more fun working with them though. There were so many clubs to work at in Vegas that their threats to go elsewhere usually fell on deaf ears.

After she put on one of her favorite clingy sequined gowns, she headed upstairs to let the deejay know she was now in the club and could be put on the stage list. Candy was proud of how hard she worked out, though dancing itself proved workout enough for most girls; even some of the scantiest outfits looked great on her body. She preferred sparkly spandex dresses the most; they made her feel sophisticated and slutty at the same time. Her nipples always popped to attention from the gentle friction of the costumes, and the customers loved watching her take the dresses off because they made her look more sophisticated than the other dancers and the slow removal of them was extremely erotic.

On her way to the deejay booth, a frequent customer, Gary, grabbed her arm, looked her in the eye, and told her he wanted the first dance because he needed to leave early to make it home by his kids' bedtime.

"Sure. Let's go upstairs right after I check in with Derek up there," Candy hollered loudly over the booming base of the music.

Luckily for him, nobody really knew Candy had arrived; otherwise there was no way he'd have been first in line. After Candy went onstage, she would pretty much spend the rest of the night in the VIP room, with the exception of her stage calls. She quickly checked in and then grabbed the customer's hand to take him upstairs to the private booths.

Though the couch dances were typically just twenty bucks per song, the house happily took five bucks from each dancer per couch dance as a rental fee. The bouncers upstairs were put in charge of tallying each girls' dances to be sure that the house got their share of the earnings. Candy happily compensated for this by up-charging her dances to twenty-five bucks. Since dancers were considered independent contractors in an all cash business and not employees of their respective clubs, it was customary for the ladies to give the house a nightly portion of their earnings (a rental fee), as well as tip the deejay and bouncers, the house mom (dressing room matron), sometimes the waitresses, and of course the IRS if the girl wanted any chance of establishing an income to purchase property or apply for credit, which most girls ignored because they didn't want or need credit. Nobody liked getting stiffed on their tips, but the house always got theirs. Since Candy was so popular, well paid, and generous, she never stiffed anyone, and the club management generally protected her from the ongoing bitchy drama of working with almost a hundred women in a small area.

As Candy and Gary entered the VIP room, they sat as far away as possible from a lady and man who were apparently trying to have sex in one of the booths. By the look of their wedding rings, they were clearly a couple, so everyone pretended not to notice. They had clearly become aroused after getting a few couch dances from some lesbian dancers.

Candy giggled at Gary, and they both just rolled their eyes at the audacity of some people. However, a few moments later a large black club bouncer named Mucho sent the couple out, explaining that the couches were not for their private liaisons but rather for the girls to work. He suggested that they might want to consider getting a room at the motel around the corner.

They were clearly bummed, but they understood and slinked away embarrassed but still very horny and quite giggly. After dancing for Gary, a blue-collar fellow who liked to hang out at the nicer clubs to stroke his ego, Candy was warmed up and ready to go onstage. The deejay knew Candy always began her shift with her favorite introductory song: "Pour Some Sugar" by Def Leppard. The song was always a sure winner with the guys, and she knew all the lyrics and moves to match the song. As the deejay announced her name, he immediately cranked up the volume, and Candy stepped onto the stage after a customer handed her a Jell-O shot to quickly gulp down. The entire crowd hollered when they saw her, though most of them wouldn't get a dance with her all night.

Derek quickly hit the smoke machine and strobe lights to make the stage and Candy the center of attention. Without hesitation, she began to leap, kick, and twirl her awesome body, which never revealed her secret addiction to Ben & Jerry's ice cream. She was completely in the moment and doing her thing. It was already hot from all the customers pressed together at small circular tables around the club. Other men stood shoulder to shoulder around the bar, smoking and drinking their beers. *This was sure to be a great night*, Candy thought. But then, out of nowhere shots rang out, and everyone hit the floor, confused. The music stopped, the house lights switched off, and then there was just smoke and darkness. Candy instinctively hit her stomach to the floor and slithered off the stage, so as not to be a focal point.

"Everybody get the hell down on the floor!" an angry man screamed, trying to disguise his heavy Hispanic accent.

Derek immediately darkened the stage lights.

"Deejay, hit them lights back on, man! It's too damned dark up in here!"

So Jazzy, the night shift manager, hit the switch on the wall that controlled the house lights. Derek had no control over the house lights, only the stage, which remained dark. Three gruff men stood at the front of the club, dressed in hospital scrubs and holding 9 mm guns. They wore nylon stocking caps over their heads. One man fired a shot at the disco globe over the stage, just to be sure they had everyone's attention. The globe exploded loudly, and glass shards came crashing to the stage floor. Everyone gasped in horror. Candy was relieved that she'd gotten off stage in time to avoid disaster. It was an unnecessary show of intimidation, but it worked quite well.

The gruff-looking men held pillowcases out and hurried around the bar, stealing customers' wallets and cash and cellphones, even their jewelry, while simultaneously collecting the same from any dancers also on the floor. There was a low mumble among the customers, but no one dared move, lest they be shot. Suddenly, Crispin appeared at the club's door. He was a beautiful man, tall and proud and almost glowing. Candy gasped as he stepped out from the shadows and simply waved his hand across the club, stilling the room, which became deafeningly silent. Everyone stared at him in horror and disbelief, especially Candy, who was now peering over the stage, hoping her new friend wouldn't get hurt.

"You guys get the hell outta here!" Crispin's voice roared over the crowded room, scaring the thugs and customers and vibrating the walls.

She found herself dumbfounded again. In his own terror, one of the thugs fired a shot at Crispin, which hit his left arm. Crispin clenched his arm and grimaced but didn't bleed or fall. Another thug shot at his chest. Crispin groaned and then clutched his chest but didn't fall. But now his face glowered with anger as he swiftly turned his head and glared at the shooters. The leader yelled to the others not to make any more shots, since it was clear they were ineffective. Who was this guy, bouncing bullets off his body like some sort of superhero, he wondered. Superman? Maybe he was an undercover cop who was wearing a vest of some sort, because it was really weird.

Meanwhile, Jazzy managed to tap the silent alarm button, which was near the light switch. *It will only be a matter of minutes before the police arrive*, he thought cleverly to himself. *If everybody just stays calm, nobody will get hurt.* As the head thug worked his way around the club, taunting and scaring the customers, he yelled at the other two thugs to move faster and waved his gun around in the air, but even he was nervous about the new visitor. He didn't want to be there all night, but there was one last thing he wanted to do: collect his niece. He'd heard she was working there now.

He walked up to one really frightened customer, put a gun barrel to his temple, and shouted and yelled obscenities at him. But Crispin appeared behind him from across the room and firmly laid his hand on the shoulder of the angry thug, who attempted to swat his hand away.

"Getcho' hands off me, mothafucka!"

Crispin did not release him but rather slowly forced the thug to his knees and firmly removed the weapon from his hand.

Despite the fact that all three of the men wore pantyhose masks over their faces to distort their looks, Gary, Candy's customer, noticed one guy was clearly missing half his ear and the leader seemed to have a heavy Hispanic accent. Gary recalled how important accurate eyewitness testimony was, since he was a fan of any kind of police investigative movies. *This info might come in handy later*, he mused. Suddenly, the leader twisted around Crispin, spotted his niece, a new dancer called Whistle, and grabbed her up off the floor. He attempted to drag her by her hair extensions into to the dressing room, but in a blur Crispin stood before them.

"I meant now!" Crispin was clear that he wasn't interested in repeating himself again. His voice resonated through the man and throughout the club. The thug dropped Whistle, unharmed to the floor.

Then another gunshot rang out. Everybody screamed, including the thug. Candy was quite puzzled as she stared at Crispin, who snatched her up off the floor and cradled her as he headed out of the club.

"I got you, babe. You're safe now." Crispin was very reassuring, and Candy was too speechless and frightened to argue.

Jazzy reached out to stop the stranger walking out with his best dancer but quickly halted when Crispin threw him a cold 'don't-fuck-with-me' stare. So he glanced at his watch. It was already 11:30 p.m. After fifteen minutes of that bullshit, where were the flipping police? If only Jazzy had known that the police had never received the alarm.

Once the thugs had scrambled out, the club finally resumed operations. Jazzy was concerned with the financial loss of the evening and decided to try to regain some profits as they waited for police, even though the crowd and dancers were too shaken up to really enjoy the show anymore. Ironically, a good crowd of customers still remained, apparently wanting to finish their expensive watered down beers before heading home and have a great story to tell to their friends at work the next day. *Thankfully no one had been harmed, much thanks to the mysterious man who showed up in the nick of time,* Jazzy thought relieved. *Hopefully, Candy made it back to work eventually unscathed*

Eventually, loud sirens broke through the music once again.

"Everyone out with your hands in the air!" yelled a policeman into a megaphone.

The music stopped for a second time that night, and the customers who'd remained slowly lined up single file by the front door with their hands in the air and then began to sit alongside the wall on the curb outside the club. Thank goodness it was a warm night.

Clearly the party was over. Jazzy was the first one out of the club and queried the police about why they had not responded sooner to the silent alarm. The police informed Jazzy that the cord to the silent alarm had most likely been severed; they had never received the alarm's signal.

The only reason they responded at all was because a customer who had been hiding in the restroom had called 911 from his cell phone. And then a second call had come in from a dancer hiding out in the dressing room downstairs.

The police then began their questioning of the customers who'd been burglarized first, since a few of them had remained at the club after Jazzy offered them free drinks. Gary, the customer who'd been standing close to the door, recalled one of the suspects had been missing half an ear; he could tell by the way the man's stocking cap had been lying against his head. He also told the police the man had a Middle Eastern accent and a peculiar body odor that he had noticed when the man pushed by him. He also mentioned that he believed the third fellow was African American because it appeared his hair had been cornrowed under his stocking cap.

It took ten grueling hours of police questioning to get through interviews of the customers, all seventy-five dancers, and the bar staff, using three separate officers. It was already late into Saturday morning when news wagons began to roll quietly into the parking lot, but no members of the media were allowed out to do interviews. The club was closed because it was now a crime scene, though thankfully nobody had been injured.

Clearly that weekend's earnings had been slaughtered, and no one knew if the club would be allowed to reopen after all this drama. The good news was that because dancers were considered independent contractors, it wouldn't be difficult for many of them to go across town and get hired by another club.

Ultimately, everyone was sent home, and the club was surrounded with police tape.

Chapter 6

After leaving the club, Diana sat huddled and scared, clutching her knees to her chest, holding a blanket Crispin had provided tightly around her body, and glancing every so often at this mysterious man, Crispin, as he sped down the Strip to his home. She wasn't sure if she should even speak to him after his bullet-bouncing demonstration.

Once they arrived, he finally looked at her and spoke quietly and evenly. "I sense your fear, but please know I have no intentions of harming you. I merely want to protect you. Besides, we haven't had our second date, yet." He smiled warmly at her with relief. "I really like the gown you're wearing tonight. I realize it's just a costume, but you look really gorgeous in it. Why don't you come inside, and I'll make us something to eat?"

Diana was slightly nervous, but considering Crispin had rescued her from harm, it seemed like an okay proposition. Besides, maybe she would find out why he felt no urgency to go to the hospital to get his wounds treated, though he didn't appear to be bleeding. Crispin walked around his car to the passenger side, where he scooped Diana up into his arms again and proceeded to carry her into his posh home.

"Oh, a girl could get used to this, Crispin. But I have to admit, you really had us all freaked out. Not more than the robbers, I mean ... but you know." Diana giggled coyly, finally speaking as he set her gently on his leather sofa.

"Well, you know with a doll like you, I could get used to this as well." Crispin winked, blushing.

His inner demon was now on full lust patrol, but he tried to contain it. It was simply thrilling to him that this gorgeous woman was now in his own home and under his spell. He wondered if she just might ask to go home. That was something he couldn't control, as determined by the power of free will. He hoped not.

"What do you propose we eat tonight?" He looked over at her from his spacious kitchen, with its black granite countertop. "I realize it's late, but I'm sure you must be hungry; I know I am. Also I'm quite the accomplished chef. So you name it, I'll cook it. I'll consider this our second date, okay?" He smiled wickedly at her again. "Imagine the serendipity of this little date."

Testing him, she replied, "I like seafood. Do you have any of that over there?" She expected him to say no, because who kept fresh seafood in their refrigerators unless they were planning on eating it soon?

"Um, actually I do. I swung by the seafood market after work today and picked up a couple of lobster tails. I was going to have some lobster tonight. I was in the mood for seafood myself. Perhaps you could stay and join me? I'd love to have your company, presuming it's not an imposition."

Diana shook her head, since a happy ending with this dashing, chivalrous man seemed inevitable. She couldn't help but notice his stark resemblance to David Beckham, the internationally-renowned soccer star turned underwear model.

"Are you kidding? I would love to stay and have some lobster with you. Do you have wine as well? I'd love to consider it our second date. I just need to call my roommate and let her know I'm all right."

"No problem, sugar. I'll just pour us some wine." Crispin gave her an evil, yet seductive smile.

Her perfume was intoxicating. Why did he have to torture himself by staying away from human women? He asked himself that question often, only to realize that his father had simply passed too soon to answer many of his questions. It saddened him sometimes. But tonight he would not allow himself to be burdened with the rules, of his kind. Diana was far too alluring for that bullshit.

After checking in with Jessie to let her know she was unharmed and in the company of the handsome man who had taken her to lunch earlier. Diana was ready to begin her little inquiry on Crispin.

"So, Crispin, that was pretty wild what you did bouncing off those bullets tonight. Are you hurt? Shouldn't we be going to the hospital? I mean, I feel bad about eating dinner if you're hurt and bleeding and all."

"No, no, sweetheart. I was wearing protection, which I've just removed. I'm gonna be just fine. Nothing but a few scratches, I'll pop a few aspirin for the discomfort, there's no need to get the hospital involved. Thanks for your concern but I'm far too distracted by you to even feel much pain, honestly." Crispin answered smoothly as he glided toward her with two wine glasses in hand. "I don't know how to explain it, but I had a funny feeling that you were in harm's way tonight. I know we don't know each other well, but I have a feeling we will."

"Wow! That's pretty wild!" Diana exclaimed. "I've never met anyone like you, but it's pretty sexy. Like Superman or something." She giggled, trying to straighten her dress.

The lobster smelled quite wonderful as it boiled in a tall kitchen stockpot.

"You don't have to fuss over that dress so much. I can promise you it won't be on much longer. I'm not capable of sitting here and watching you eat in that tight, clingy, see-through dress and not wanting to unleash my passion upon you. You realize seafood is an aphrodisiac, don't you?" Crispin looked at her seductively. As he spoke, he gently grabbed Diana by the hand and pulled her close to him. She was now straddling him as much as her clingy dress would allow. "Yeah," he murmured, "this is already better than a couch dance at the club."

Then his hands tightly gripped her round, firm behind, and he thrust his tongue deeply into her mouth. Crispin's erection was at full attention, as were Diana's nipples. Just then the alarm sounded to pull the lobster from the boiling water on the stove.

"Oh damn," Diana blurted out. "It was just getting good." Pouting, she slowly moved from Crispin's lap so he could attend to the lobster.

"Don't you worry, pretty woman. I'll be right back. Crispin excused himself from her embrace and reassured her of his immediate return with the lobster and more wine. Diana was already so aroused by him that she, also quickly excused herself to the restroom so she could remove the thong she'd worn to work in and discreetly stuff into her mini purse she always carried around the floor at work, for she had every intention of screwing him tonight. If seafood was an aphrodisiac, she was sure going to test that theory. She grinned to herself.

When she returned, she wrapped herself in the fuzzy animal print throw that lay over the back of the sofa. Crispin was all too happy to plop back onto the couch next to Diana, where they proceeded to rip and tear away at the freshly prepared lobster and dip it in the buttery sauce Crispin had prepared for them. *It was simply delicious*, Diana thought.

As Crispin poured more wine into their glasses, he chuckled and asked Diana, "So, Miss Candy, where will you be working at from now on? It doesn't look like your club's going to be open for a while."

She frowned and replied, "Yeah, right. I know. Tonight really sucked for work, it was by far, the shortest shift I've ever worked." Then she mumbled aloud, her mouth betraying her thoughts, " But, I suppose everything happens for a reason." She pouted while rolling her eyes toward the ceiling wearing a mischievous grin and winking at Crispin.

"No, no, I'm sorry. I didn't mean to get you all down about it," Crispin sputtered, interrupting her thoughts.

"That's okay. Don't be sorry. I'm gonna have to think about it eventually anyway. The truth is, unlike many of the girls I work with, I actually have a savings account that I keep for unfortunate events such as this, or for the flu or something. You just never know with this job. It's not like we get sick days or disability or anything." They both chuckled at the ludicrousness.

As Crispin headed back into the kitchen for another bottle of wine,

Diana took the opportunity to glance around his lovely home. She couldn't help but notice several Bibles lying around.

"Can you please explain the Bibles lying around your house? It seems a bit creepy to me, not that I've got anything personal against the Bible other than its got some pretty entertaining stories. After all, I did attend Catholic schools for most of my life."

"Well, it's kind of a long story," Crispin said.

"Provided you don't turn out to be some weirdo serial killer and I have to kill you and run out of here, I plan on staying for dessert. Besides, it sounds pretty interesting. Obviously I'm not working right now, so I've got plenty of time." Diana laid back deeper into the sofa, indicating that she had time to listen.

"Great. Well, I'm definitely not a serial killer!" Crispin couldn't help but laugh aloud. If only she could read his mind and know his true game plan. "It's complicated," he started again. "I don't how much of a Bible scholar you are, Diana, but there is a race of people briefly described in the scriptures as Nephilim. Apparently they were a race of giants. Anyhow, many years ago, before he passed on, my father told me that our ancestors go back as far as the scriptures and this particular race of people, the Nephilim, as the myth goes, with the exception that we're obviously not giants. I never really believed him, but one day curiosity got the best of me, and I began to study it for myself; so I have kept a lot of his research information downstairs in the storage room in my basement. I wish there was more information in all these bibles I have lying around. I have every version ever written and still, nothing.

"Since then I've become a bit obsessed with finding out more about who these people were. The Bible doesn't say much about them, which is why we're a myth. I suppose it's a bit strange that I have so many Bibles lying about, considering I'm an atheist, but I assure you it's only for research, and I spend lots of time at the library. Trust me, I'm not a Bible-thumper."

Then Crispin shrugged, as if to say, *That's all.* "Now if you don't mind, I think we should discuss something far more interesting. Like us, right now." He licked his lips and strolled across the room toward her.

He was simply drop-dead gorgeous, Diana thought quietly as she watched him swagger across the room, holding a wine bottle and wearing his megawatt smile. "Diana had become used to seeing hot guys in the club, many of whom were professional athletes, but there was something different about Crispin and she couldn't understand her fascination and attraction towards him even if his descendants did seem creepy to her. "Well Crispin, you're right, that is an interesting revelation and if I knew more about the world of the supernatural I would probably be pretty freaked out by you, but lucky for both us right now, I'm not. Strange is the name of the game, in my world, but so far you seem to be a pretty decent guy, to me anyway"; so she appeared to seem unfazed by his admission.

Diana didn't want to come off as completely insensitive, so she followed up with, "Have you learned much yet?" And she showed some interest, though even after ten years of Catholic school education, none of it really rang a bell. The only giant that came to mind was Goliath and the story of the little boy, David, who killed him with his slingshot.

"No, not a lot really. It's just a personal project of mine, and there seems to be a lot of speculation and myth on the subject; it's hard to know what to believe. Genesis chapter 6, is all I really can find in the scriptures, which is why we're considered a myth, since there's so much debate over what it really means. I wish my father was still around to help me because Ancestry.com isn't going to help me at all", then he chuckled. Now let's change the subject to dessert. Are you an ice cream or cheesecake fan?" Crispin's eyes glowed brightly. He was, desperate to change the subject, not wanting to arouse her suspicions any longer.

"I'm definitely a cheesecake girl, although I admit that after working all night, my roommate and I occasionally enjoy indulging in a pint of Ben & Jerry's ice cream." Diana laughed loudly and then gulped down some more wine.

Crispin laughed with her and then said, "There's no way to tell from the looks of you that you are a Ben & Jerry's ice cream junkie. But I enjoy a girl who's not afraid to indulge a little. Shall we toast to indulgence?"

They clinked glasses and smiled at each other. Diana was really beginning to get comfortable and cozy with Crispin. But Crispin was pure evil personified. He knew he didn't have much time to make his play.

"Do you have a boyfriend?" he asked her, already knowing the answer but wanting to appear ignorant.

"No, I'm really not that interested in anyone right now. But of course, that could all change tonight, right?" she teased back, winking.

"I have every intention of changing your status after tonight," he replied salaciously.

"You can probably imagine that this is a tough profession to maintain a solid relationship in," she spoke dryly.

Crispin was definitely a good-looking guy, Diana thought; and funny too. Maybe she should have asked if he was single as well, though it didn't appear as if he shared his home with anyone. He wasn't wearing a ring, but she knew better than to think that meant anything. Heck, for all she knew his wife could be out of town on business. Married guys were by far the worst flirts and infidels, and they were always on the lookout for the next pretty young thing. That was what the business had taught her anyway. *Oh well, what's the harm in asking?*

"So, Crispin, what about you? Do you live in this fabulous home all alone?"

"Unfortunately, yes, I live all alone. I don't see anyone seriously either. My career requires long hours, plus my business phone in my home/office rings constantly and most ladies are just too intolerant of my ever-changing schedule. It's not that I haven't tried. Much like you."

Diana began to relax a bit more. Staring into Crispin's eyes was quite frankly making her feel pretty aroused. He mentioned that many of the ladies who were most interested wanted a father figure for their kids and a husband with a solid career. So he said he'd resorted to casual dating instead of getting too serious or involved with anyone. He had no children (didn't like them and didn't want them), no ex-girlfriends running about town, and a very respectable career in the works with hopes of one day starting his own firm. He really desired to be in a monogamous relationship with someone, but it hadn't happened yet, and it could be very complicated considering his aspirations. Diana could see he was a good catch. He was young and handsome, had a professional career, and was not easily intimidated by some of her off-hand and somewhat blunt comments, which he laughed about, or her incessant potty mouth. Conversation was easy with Crispin.

Diana excused herself to the restroom once more to check her face and hair as well as peek to see if there were any remnants of another woman's presence. His home was simply lovely. Clearly it was professionally cleaned, since a guy with his erratic schedule probably didn't have time to come home and vacuum, dust, and mop his floors. The restroom was done in black marble, with a black and white marble large checkered floor. This guy certainly hadn't cut corners when it had come to building his house; he was no cheapskate, that was for sure.

When she looked into the mirror, she noticed a pink glow in her face, probably because he made her blush. She was already crushing on this guy. Even if he turned out to be a dud, at least she could get laid by a hot guy tonight, she figured. Well, it wasn't as if he wasn't a Greek god. Why had he never gotten a dance with her before tonight? What was the story with that?

Crispin seemed delighted again when she returned. "I was beginning to miss you," he said sweetly.

Diana leaned over the sofa and gave him a quick peck on the cheek. "You've abducted me from my job, silly. I don't even have my car here. What did you expect me to do, leap from the bathroom window and go running down the street in high heels and a see-through dress, looking like a hooker or something?"

Crispin just smiled coyly, blushed, and pulled her into his lap. "I thought you might want to escape my boring conversation," he teased her.

He didn't want to seem presumptuous, and the demon inside him continued to admonish him, but so far Diana's lifestyle looked pretty good as well: no children, no ex-husband or old boyfriends, a college degree, professional parents, clearly a great body and face, and finally, another soul to possess. Diana seemed different to him, however, he wasn't certain that he wanted to victimize her. He was already having mixed feelings for her. She seemed like a possible great girlfriend candidate, actually. He was beginning to see how his father may have been lured into a relationship with his human mother. He began to feel slightly guilty for even considering wanting to hurt her.

When they were finished with dinner, Crispin got up casually. "Shall I start a fresh pot of coffee, because I have a feeling we might be up for a while?"

"That would be awesome if you don't mind. The wine is fabulous, but I do believe coffee goes better with cheesecake." She smiled coyly at him.

"No, no, sweetheart, it's no bother at all. It's my pleasure now that you've allowed me to kidnap you from work; hopefully you didn't sneak away to the bathroom to call the police. So of course your wish is my command." Crispin smiled broadly as Diana shook her head at him about calling the police.

"No, Crispin, no police, not yet, anyway," she giggled at him. "Thank you, for the coffee, by the way" she murmured.

"You are very welcome," he replied, handing her a cup and saucer. Next he sat a small tray of cream and sugar on the coffee table in front of them. "And what a fabulous surprise date, I might add. I think I showed up just in time." He went on to explain to Diana that she was not only easy on the eye but full of all sorts of knowledge on sports, cars, celebrity gossip, politics, and the latest breaking news. It was not typical—a news-watching stripper.

Diana confessed that she watched a lot of TV and read many celebrity magazines and books (she'd gotten into the habit during college) when she wasn't working to keep her in the loop. She was flattered and found herself becoming even more attracted to Crispin. *He was very tall but not a giant at six foot four, deeply tanned, athletically built, thirty years old, and very bright. Not to mention he had a financially stable occupation as an accountant and financial advisor, so he wouldn't be envious of her income or expect her to pay his bills,* she thought. But it was safer to brush that thought away.

Not too bad for a babe like him. I'm sure he's got a dozen girls trying to bag him, though, she thought, but she wasn't a stranger to competition, and she rarely let it concern her. Just as she was pondering that idea, he gently grabbed her around her waist, pulled her towards him, and planted a long passionate kiss on her lips. He held her so closely that she could feel the arousal in his pants. Diana felt herself becoming slightly dizzy as Crispin's gaze squarely met hers.

"I want to take you to bed. I just can't tolerate looking at you in this dress anymore. Please, forgive me. I hope that wasn't too forward. I think my mouth betrayed my brain," he whispered seductively to her.

"Wow! That's exactly what I was thinking," she sputtered. "What are we waiting for? We've had lobster, wine, cheesecake, coffee, and some hella conversation. We've been here for over two hours laughing and talking already! I say it's time to celebrate!"

Crispin grinned brightly and then helped her up from his plush sofa. "My room is just down this short hallway, and you should know there hasn't been a woman in here for over a year, so I may seem a little ambitious between the sheets," he lied, as he certainly enjoyed the company of escorts now and again.

Diana was quite excited. She felt her nipples harden when Crispin took her elbow and escorted her down the hallway. "I think I find that a bit hard to believe with your drop-dead good looks." She winked at him in disbelief.

They entered his massive bedroom suite with its circular bed, silver and black tapestry, and shiny statues placed strategically throughout the room. *He was gorgeous, with impeccable taste for interior design,* Diana thought.

"Wow! I love your room!" she exclaimed.

"Thanks, I kind of designed it myself using some suggestions from an interior designer friend whose taxes I did a few years ago." Crispin quickly skipped across the room and turned on the electric fireplace to set the ambience. Soon he was back by her side and ready to get intimate. "Do you prefer to be called Candy or your real name, Diana?" He questioned while nuzzling her neck with feather-light kisses.

"Well, my good friends just call me Di, actually." She giggled and kissed him back.

"Well then, I think I'd like to be considered a good friend." He chuckled, pulling her body closer to him.

"Um, do you have condoms?" Diana questioned as she wriggled away slightly. Concerned, she looked at his face.

"Actually, I do. I bought a fresh box recently in case I got lucky, which I never do, I'm very particular, you know" he lied. "But it seemed a good idea anyway. They're right over there in my night table." He smiled lustfully at her.

"Well good. I think you're about to get lucky then," Diana responded, relieved. Then she snapped her game face on. "If you want me to dance for you, then you're going to have to provide some music, lover boy." She winked and gently began to sway her hips.

"Music won't be a problem, baby doll. I just need to reach over there and grab the right remote." Crispin reached over to the vacant night table, where a plethora of remotes lay in a decorative metal basket, and grabbed the remote for his built-in Bose sound system. "What do you want to hear, honey buns? I've got rock 'n' roll, pop hits, slow jams, or I can shuffle them. Whatever works for you." He was clearly far more excited about the dance than he was the music anyway.

"May I suggest the slow jams first and then the shuffle? I can move to anything, honestly. I'm not intimidated by any music except heavy metal, but let's just take it slow first." Diana stared at him.

They were both burning with lust and desire. Crispin was becoming impatient, but he maintained his easy, laid-back disposition.

"Slow jams it is, honey. No bouncers, no customers, no distractions, no deejay. Only me," Crispin said, gladly aiming the remote toward his hidden sound system.

Immediately, Beyonce's "If I Were a Boy" began to play in the room.

"I totally love this song." Diana gleamed and began to dance in front of Crispin, who lay back on his chaise lounge. He could barely contain himself as he watched her *slowly caress* her breasts and thighs, while maintaining perfect rhythm. *She clearly was a professional*, he thought while being mesmerized.

This man is so ungodly gorgeous, she thought. She could barely control the moisture between her thighs as she watched him carefully examine her every sultry move. Simultaneously, Crispin began to stroke himself outside his slacks while grinning, moaning, and enjoying the show. He was beside himself with his dumb luck at popping into the club to visit tonight. What a perfect surprise ending, he thought. Tonight was going to be good after all.

"You know, Di, I don't keep a no-touch policy here in my home. So please, don't slap me if I decide to touch you, okay?" he teased.

"Oh no, honey, quite the contrary, Crispin. I think I might be offended if you didn't," she teased back and giggled.

Chapter 8

After a long night of passionate sex, in which Crispin occasionally let her come up for air before he was ready to go again, Diana awoke to another bright sunny day in Las Vegas. She decided to head home to her condo, which was not far from the Strip. Crispin, however, was not quite ready for Diana to hurry off.

"Hey gorgeous," he whispered to her in a raspy morning voice. "Let me at least make you to breakfast. I mean, you must be famished after last night, right?" He pulled on her as she attempted to get up from his cozy bed.

"Gosh, Crispin, don't make this harder than it already is. Of course I could lie here in your arms all day long and just check out on the entire day, having embarrassing amounts of sex." She winked at him as she hurried off to the restroom, hoping to wash the makeup off her face and rinse out her mouth.

"Hey, that's a great idea, Diana; let's just blow off the entire day. We could both call in sick and just hang out together. We'll do whatever comes to mind! I'm jealous. Hmm, why didn't I think of that first?"

Before she knew it, he was up out of bed and happily standing naked in front of her, his morning arousal at full attention and waiting to greet her once again. *Oh shit*, Diana thought, *I'm such a sucker, but I must force myself to leave.*

"See, my friend and I are so excited to have you stay and play." Crispin reached out to her, wearing his megawatt smile, and pulled her to him. Clutching her very tightly and nuzzling her hair, he gripped her buttocks and forced his arousal against her thigh. It was simply too much for her wanton body to bear.

"Okay, just a little longer, Crispin. "You're obviously an animal in bed, I probably should've taken my vitamins yesterday! But then I need to shower and get home before my roommate burns our house down while she's busy fucking her boyfriend, Chad. By the way, you do realize that today is Saturday. You rescued me last night, Friday, so it's not necessary for you to call in sick. I'm not scheduled to work until eight, but I have a ton of errands to run today before work."

By the time Crispin and Diana completed their morning sexercise, it was already ten in the morning. Diana looked curiously at Crispin and said, "You are a phenomenal lover, even in the morning, so I find it hard to believe that you're not seeing anyone seriously. I wonder if you're being honest with me."

Crispin propped himself up on his elbow and grinned, looking down at her, replied, "*Hmm*, thank you, Diana, but do you recall the phone ringing while you were here last night? Or this morning even? Did you hear the doorbell chime? There's no one else in my busy life right now. You'll just have to trust me on that, sweetheart. Poor me, I'm so lonely. But I could easily say the same about you as well."

With that, Diana nodded and hopped back up, feeling completely spent from the intense workout that Crispin had given her last night. "You know what just occurred to me, Crispin? I don't have my clothes here, and I've got to meet Jackie, my trainer, today. You carried me from the club last night in my slinky see-through dress, which I cannot wear home or to the gym."

"Yeah, you're right. But that's all right. I've got some sweats and a T-shirt you can wear home, and it will give me another reason to see you; so I can get my clothes back." He chuckled.

"Hey, thanks. That's really cool of you! I'll go take a shower while you find me something to wear home!" Diana was thrilled to have met a guy whose clothes she could wear again. It had always been so cool to wear Ryan's clothes; he was her last boyfriend. By this time she was certain that she would see Crispin again. He made it very clear that he was excited by her presence.

Diana thoroughly enjoyed Crispin's modern shower, which had jets shooting out from all the walls. It was so relaxing that she began daydreaming and almost forgot to wash herself, but finally the shampoo appeared before her blurry, wet gaze and the body wash as well. It wasn't her own stuff, but it would have to do for now. Besides, she might enjoy spending the rest of the afternoon smelling like freshly washed Crispin.

Crispin was in the bathroom, holding a big fluffy towel for her as she stepped out of the shower. She hadn't even heard him slip into the bathroom. Of course, one of the benefits of being part supernatural; the ability to essentially become invisible at will and be extra quiet when sneaking around.

"I realize we both have things to do today, but I just hate to see you leave." He spoke quietly, his voice sexy and somewhat forlorn as he pulled her in close with the towel. He was aroused again.

This time Diana was stalwart, freshly showered and ready to get going on the day. It was obvious that Crispin could be a distraction. Besides, sleeping with her seemed to be his biggest motivation for seeing her again, though he would never say so. She had to admit that sleeping with him was exactly the medicine she needed last night and this morning to free her thoughts of the horrible break-in at the club, the previous night. Crispin politely handed her a small stack of his clothing to wear back home. Diana took them gratefully and quickly began to dress while he watched her, frowning. Crispin's clothing was a bit large on her but they felt good and looked good all the same, unfortunately she didn't have a bra with her, but she'd just have to go without. Her hair was wet, so she tossed it into a ponytail, so that it wouldn't be in her face preparing it for her workout. Crispin enjoyed watching her, but quickly realized that he needed to get dressed too. He grabbed a pair of jeans off of a chair by his desk and quickly pulled them on. Next he through on a sweatshirt with letters the UNLV clearly printed in bold, red letters across the front. He slipped into his gym shoes and was ready to go, but first he invited her to brunch, and she happily agreed. Diana watched him as well. *It's nice to see him in something other than a suit,* she thought to herself.

"Let's go, Crispin. We can't hang out here all day, though I enjoy snuggling with you. Can you run me back to the club to get my truck now, please?"

"Actually, I thought we'd go and grab some brunch first, since it is getting kind of late. Obviously you wouldn't allow me you take to breakfast today, but I'm glad you reconsidered getting a bite with me because I'm famished after last night's exercise with you." Crispin smiled broadly at her again. *He looks good even in the morning, sure wish I did,* she grinned to herself.

He's great! Plus he's handsome too, Diana thought coyly. "I'll tell you what. Why don't we go pick up my truck first, and then I'll meet up with you for lunch?"

"Cool. That sounds like a deal." Crispin nodded, satisfied with that proposal. Then he grabbed his car keys, went to the front door, and held it open for his new friend.

Chapter 9

Diana happily collapsed into the bucket seat of Crispin's Corvette, thoroughly exhausted after several hours of sex and private couch dances for Crispin the previous night. She pointed to a blue Jeep sitting in his driveway, as if to suggest someone had stopped by. He quickly explained it away as his other, less flashy car. She smiled in agreeance. Then she recalled that as she danced for him, he had lined her G-string with fifty dollar bills, hoping to make the night not a total loss for her. *How generous of him*, she thought. But now the fun was over, and it was time to get busy on the days' errands.

As they turned into the club, their mouths dropped open in shock and surprise. The driver's side window of Diana's Hummer had been smashed in with a large object. Crispin quickly parked, and they both jumped out of his car and hurried over to her vehicle as fast as they could. Once they arrived at the window, they saw a brick lying on the driver's seat.

"Oh my God! I should've stayed! *Maybe someone would have heard the noise and come outside to investigate!*"

"Come on, Diana, if you'd have stayed it could have been a whole lot worse. You may have been killed! We can fix the window, babe, but not you. Shit, I'm still really sorry about this. Please don't cry. Come here." Crispin pulled her close to hug and console her. Out of Diana's sight, his eyes turned black with demonic vengeance "We need to file a police report right now, though I doubt it'll do us any good, but I think I saw the fellas responsible for this. I saw some guys messing around in the parking lot when I pulled in last night, before the burglary and when I got out of my car, they ran away, but I got a good look at them."

"Maybe if I had just stayed here," Diana began, "this wouldn't have happened. Besides, the club has cameras on the lot. Maybe they saw something. I don't know. Ugh, this really pisses me off! Dammit, doesn't anybody have a conscience anymore?"

She sighed, but she knew Crispin was right; she could've been seriously hurt. Diana looked up into Crispin's eyes, which were now bright green and alert again. She pulled out her cell phone and dialed the police department; they said they would send someone over as soon as possible. Crispin and Diana decided to wait inside his convertible with the air conditioning on after driving around the corner and grabbing a couple of Slurpees. They laughed and talked for about forty-five minutes until the patrol car finally appeared. They immediately exited Crispin's vehicle and headed over to the Hummer to meet the officer.

"Wow, this club has been a busy place in the last twenty-four hours, huh?" the officer started. "I'm sorry. I'm Officer Maria Sanchez. I was dispatched to take your report." Officer Sanchez stuck out her hand and gave them both a firm handshake. They introduced themselves as well.

Diana began the story of what they had encountered when they arrived, and then Crispin quickly jumped in, completing the story and giving an expert description of the alleged suspects. Diana was in complete shock and awe at his descriptions, which included details about their tattoos, and so was the officer.

"Well," said Officer Sanchez, "one thing is for sure: it is very difficult to get accurate eye witness descriptions of the suspects, but you must have a photographic memory because that was damn good. Maybe you should have been a cop. Make sure you give your insurance company a call, and here's my card if you need anything else. These crimes are not always quickly resolved, if at all, but I'll make sure to stay in contact with you, and here's your report number on the back of my card for your insurance company. I'm very sorry about this, but try to enjoy the rest of your day. Don't let the bad guys win!" Officer Sanchez smiled weakly and then headed back to her cruiser.

"Thank you very much, ma'am," Diana said softly.

Crispin turned toward her and gave her a big hug. She could hear his stomach grumbling.

"All righty. Now I'm thoroughly famished. Can we go eat, please?" he begged.

"Sure," said Diana, "but let me get my truck out of this parking lot. I'll meet you around the corner at Denny's. I'll just roll both windows down. But at least it will be in my custody. *Ugh!*"

Several minutes later, as Diana and Crispin sat facing each other at a small table, they both quickly ordered from the anxious waitress standing nearby and eagerly flirting with Crispin.

Crispin reached across the table and held Diana's hands. Then he looked deeply into her eyes. Speaking softly, he said, "Diana, I have really enjoyed the time we spent together last night. I feel like we have a lot in common, and I could really dig hanging out with somebody like you. I would really enjoy getting to know you better. What do you think about that?" He smiled proudly.

He then looked down at the table, his eyes blackening once again, this time with lust and control. He knew he needed to seal the deal with Diana before she was out of his power again. Knowing that possession could only occur if a soul invited it meant more manipulation on his part. Although he felt certain that Diana was falling for him, he still needed her consent to possess her soul. He would simply need to be patient and bide his time.

"Crispin, I've been thinking about us all day, and last night it was great sharing your lobster, cheesecake, and wine. And the sex— was simply outrageous. I could really see myself falling hard for you, but then I'd be crushed when you left me. Besides, how do I know you don't just want me for my body? Everything always seems so cool in the beginning, but then my job always becomes the issue, and I don't want to be hurt again." Diana apologized. "Crispin, I'm not exactly the type of girl you'd want to take home to meet your mother. You're so hot and successful. Why do you want to be with an exotic dancer when you could have anybody? I mean, I'm no schlep, but you know, I come with baggage." Just then the waitress appeared with their food, setting their plates down slowly, so as to stare at Crispin a bit longer. They both thanked her proceeded to eat while continuing their discussion. Crispin let go of her hands to indulge in his fries.

"Yeah, me too, Diana. Thank you, but that's my point. I'm perfectly secure in myself, my looks, and my abilities. I don't dread what others think of me. That's so high school. I'm grown now. I can 'like' whomever I choose. I choose you, and you being a dancer doesn't make me like you any less, okay? I know it's just your job, and I'm pretty certain it's temporary, besides you don't exactly strike as a girl who has self-esteem issues and is overly needy."

"You say that now, but, Crispin, but we've only spent one night together. You don't know me well enough yet." Diana reached across the table, took his hands, and smiled softly. "All you really know is that I'm an exotic dancer, and that I also graduated from UNLV I can see from your shirt that, maybe you went there as well. I don't smoke, I'm a social drinker at best, and I love to work out! I'm pretty certain that's not much to build a relationship on, and besides, how much do I know about you? I know you're thirty years old, you have a great budding career in finance, you have no wife and no children, that you know of anyway, and of course you rock between the sheets. Oh yeah, I forgot to mention you're an atheist, which is weird to me because I've never met an atheist, with bibles lying about their house." Diana watched Crispin's facial expressions and grinned, picking up another french fry and biting into it.

"So far so good, Diana, but the part about taking you to meet my mother is wrong; she died during childbirth with me." He displayed a grim smile and slowly shook his head.

Her smile immediately turned upside down. "Oh shit, Crispin, I'm so sorry. I didn't realize. I shouldn't have been so insensitive."

Diana felt saddened and shameful at the same time. She imagined how horrific that day must have been for his father, having to take the baby home instead of the baby's mother and deal with the loss of his wife. How could someone rejoice and mourn all at once? She reached over and squeezed Crispin's hand again.

"Diana, it's okay. Don't be sorry. You didn't know about that, but if we were together, you would learn all of that and more about me. Please, just go with it. Don't worry. I'm not like other guys you've dated. Trust me. I promise you. But I probably should follow you home so I'll at least know where you live. I promise never to hurt you. I'm certain you've heard that before, but I urge you to give me a chance, clearly I'm not happy being alone all the time."

Diana looked at Crispin with mild unertainty but then smiled in agreement. "Okay, Crispin. Let's give it a try," she finally agreed, unaware of the consequences. Secretly she was thrilled to have a boyfriend who was much smarter and better looking than her roommate's.

With that, Crispin went up to the register to pay their bill and they both headed back outside smiling and rubbing their full stomachs. Crispin would follow Diana home and then they could begin to run their respective errands. They agreed to try to get together later on. Diana figured as long as she rode around town with both front windows down, nobody would be aware of the damage to her vehicle, after she'd swept most of the shattered glass off into the parking lot and floor. Before going home, she headed straightaway to her local Hummer dealership and made a damage report, as well as called her insurance carrier.

Crispin was pleased to wait patiently for her in the parking area. Ironically, the body of her Hummer hadn't been damaged and neither had the expensive Bose sound system; it just appeared to have been a random act of violence. After that, Diana headed back to her condo to grab a protein shake and her workout gear hoping Jessie and Chad had left the place still standing. She gave Jessie a call to let her know that she had made it home safely, so she need not worry about her after what had happened at the club, she'd had the pleasure of spending the night with Crispin, who'd rescued her and taken her back to his place. Jessie was quite pumped to meet Diana's new boyfriend since she hadn't had one for so long. Then she hurried off the phone, as she and Chad were on their way somewhere.

"Diana, that's so cool! Is he hot? OMG, Di! I can't wait to meet him. Then Chad won't feel so lonely when he comes over because there'll be another guy to talk to!"

"Yeah, I know, right?" Diana retorted, wrinkling her face at the thought of Crispin and Chad having anything in common. Just then her call waiting beeped. It was her father.

"Oh my God, Dad, you're not going to believe what happened to my Hummer last night! Some dumb guys were screwing off in the parking lot last night while I was working and threw a brick through my window. I'm so pissed. Thank goodness my boyfriend, Crispin, got a really good look at the guys when he was dropping by to see me, so he gave the officer a description of the possible suspects for me. I've been by the dealership to order a new window and already filed a claim with my insurance company. Now I'm off to the gym and then post office and of course my weekly visit to the Laundromat. Big yay!" Diana exclaimed sarcastically as she continued speeding down the road, too fast as usual.

"Well, I'm sorry to hear about your club and your car, but it sounds like you're okay and took care of matters efficiently. No doubt life is full of surprises as well as boring tasks that still have to be taken care of, honey, even when drama has happened in our lives. I'm going to run by the house a bit later today after my rounds and check in on your mother and give her your latest updates. I get concerned when I haven't heard from you in a while," her father said calmly. "So love you much, sugar. Call you later, and sorry about your truck. We'll get it all fixed up again. More importantly, you're okay. Don't worry your pretty little head about it."

"Thanks, Daddy. Love you, too. Talk to you later."

After entering through the security gates, Diana and Crispin finally arrived at her condo on the edge of town. Once they'd parked and left their vehicles, Crispin took her hand and commented.

"Well, this is quite a nice place out here, Diana, safely away from the nonsense of downtown Vegas." Crispin appeared pleased that Diana was safely tucked away from some of the goofballs she often danced for. "I'm not really sure what I was expecting. Something nice, I guess, because you strike me as a classy lady."

Diana was happy to see that Crispin approved of her humble place, which was quietly nestled in a wooded area off a golf course. Her father had helped her secure it by cosigning for her. After she and Crispin approached the door and swung it open to the foyer, they were surprised to see that they had a small audience of Jessie, Chad, and Sister Lori, who Diana had forgotten she agreed to meet with.

"Hi, everyone," she called out and smiled, waving at them all. Chad, I'm glad you're all here to meet my new boyfriend." She went about the business of introducing Crispin to each person in the room and then turned to Lori and apologized that she'd forgotten about their meeting today. She asked Sister Lori if she had been waiting long because she'd had some unexpected drama with her car that morning and had forgotten about their meeting, otherwise she'd have called.

"Oh, no, that's fine Diana, I haven't been waiting long, as a matter of fact I had forgotten about our meeting, too, so I was running late myself", Lori smiled.

Crispin and Sister Lori's eyes locked swiftly, and his eyes became black once again as they glared at one another. This time everyone witnessed it, including Diana.

"Oh dear, Crispin, come over here. Sit down and watch the game with Chad. I'll grab you a beer from the fridge. Are you all right?" Diana asked him as he sat down in a comfortable leather chair by the television. He urged her not to take too long because they had things to do still. Honestly, Crispin wasn't happy about Diana hanging out with a clergy member.

"Yeah, yeah, I'm fine, baby. She just caught me off guard, and sometimes I'm overprotective. She strikes me as someone who's up to something. Besides, you know how I feel about religion," Crispin whispered to her.

Diana quickly grabbed a beer from the fridge and ran it over to him; he was thankful and quickly got into the game with Chad. Diana nodded and straightaway motioned Sister Lori outside onto her balcony for some lemonade and small chat, curious about her motives.

"I'm sorry about that," Sister Lori began. "Sometimes my habit outfit spooks people, but it's more official looking and respectful, even when it's terribly hot outside like today." She took a shaky sip of lemonade. "So," she began, "how long have you and that young man been dating if you don't mind me asking?" She pulled a handkerchief from her purse and dabbed the perspiration from her nose and forehead.

Diana quickly lied to save face. "We've been dating for a couple of weeks now. Not long," she assured her. She wondered where this conversation was going. In an effort to change the subject quickly, she asked Sister Lori, "Did you just pop in to introduce yourself to me, or were you going to attempt to do a Bible study on me? I don't see your Bible. Can I presume it's not a Bible study then?"

"No, dear. I'm not here for a Bible study, only to introduce myself in case you ever have any questions and you don't want to speak to a stranger. You have a lovely view out here, by the way," Sister Lori replied, motioning to the pond but still seeming distracted by Crispin as she repeatedly checked over her shoulder. "You know, Diana, the spirit gives some individuals special gifts, and it has been revealed to me that I have the gift of discernment, which essentially means that I can sense things about people that others may miss. Now, I don't expect you to take this kindly, but your boyfriend, Crispin, has an evil spirit about him, which he knew I sensed immediately. That's why his eyes turned black when he stared at me."

"Hold on, Sister Lori!" Diana exclaimed in an excited whisper, grabbing the nun's arm. "Are you saying that Crispin is not who he says he is? You don't even know him! He's one of the best, kindest guys I've ever known!" She laughed at the absurdity of such a comment from Sister Lori. Then she looked at her seriously and exclaimed, " I'm appalled that you should come to my house the first time and accuse my boyfriend whom you don't even know. I'm seriously considering asking you to leave, but out of respect for my mother I won't. He's been so kind and generous; I'm having a hard time believing you. As a matter of fact I just plain refuse to believe you!" Diana plopped back into her seat and pondered, "However, he did mention his ancestors went back to the Bible days. The Nephilim, I believe. But, he hasn't given me a minute alone to look up the myth or legend. But still, I can't believe your boldness. You've got some nerve, lady."

"Well, I don't know what or who he says he is, but a 'good guy' is not one of them. That's for sure. Especially the Nephilim. Many of us still believe they walk among us in human form and excel in all forms of carnal hedonism. I don't know much more. Most Christian circles refuse to even discuss them, refuting them as simple myth and folklore. Perhaps you could try someone over at the university," Sister Lori scoffed.

"Last night my club was broken into, and he mysteriously showed up and rescued me!" Diana stared at Sister Lori incredulously. "Why would he rescue me if he's a bad guy?" She was amazed at Sister Lori's insight, so she decided to take her business card, return to the group, and call Sister Lori later.

Diana walked Sister Lori quickly out to her light blue Volkswagen Beetle. "Hey, Sister Lori, thanks for coming by today. I apologize for my tardiness again, yet you've managed to scare the shit out of me now! I'm not totally convinced that there's something diabolical about Crispin, yet. I plan on enjoying him until he gives me reason enough not to." She chuckled softly and winked at her.

Sister Lori rolled down her window and said, "Crispin may appear to be a good catch, but be careful with him. Ultimately things are not always what they appear. Never judge a book by its cover, honey. He wants you for more than your mind or body, maybe even for your soul. I don't know how much you know about him, but find out as much as you can," Sister Lori warned her and swiftly drove off.

Diana managed to put on her poker face and headed back into the living area, where the others were watching the game. "Hey, Crispin, let us retire back to my room for a little while." She knew she needed to try to distract him if she was going to do what Sister Lori suggested.

Crispin took her hand and gladly followed, excusing himself from his company.

"Oh yeah, Diana, your bedroom looks so comfy." Crispin immediately went over to her bed and collapsed onto it. "I feel like a nap. Want to take one with me now that Sister What's Her Face is gone?"

"Uh, yeah, that's fine. I'm a bit tired myself." Diana figured she should at least give Crispin the benefit of the doubt as she learned more about him.

"Hey, so what was that lady doing here? Does she come over a lot?" Crispin began to sound nervous and very concerned, extremely human.

"No. Actually, that was the first time I'd ever met her. She's a friend of my mother's, and ever since I began dancing, my mom always sends her church lady friends by to check on me and to pray for me. Sometimes they like to do a Bible study." She attempted to sound more composed.

"Oh, I see. So she wants to make sure you don't befriend the wrong kinds of people then." He seemed pleased with that response and less wary now, although he was certain he wouldn't be spending much time around the sister because she might very well expose him.

"Yeah, pretty much that's all." She smiled, knowing Sister Lori had warned her about getting to know him better. "It was pretty obvious that you didn't seem too thrilled to see her though, because your eyes got all dark and scary like. I'm sorry I forgot I was supposed to meet her today. I don't want you to ever feel uncomfortable in my home," Diana stroked his hair and teased him a little and making him laugh to lighten the conversation again.

"You know, Crispin, I feel like we have so much to learn about each other yet. It seems like we like lots of the same things, from fast cars and motorcycles to roller coasters, but I don't know very much about you personally. I mean, you mentioned you had some mysterious lineage to some tribe of giants in the Bible. I know we obviously don't feel the same about religion, because I'm certainly not an atheist. I really can't even begin to understand it, especially when I saw so many Bibles at your house. It just seems really weird, that's all." Diana scrunched her face at the mere thought of it.

"Diana, I own a cottage up at Lake Tahoe that could use some company. Maybe we could head up there and spend an entire weekend just getting to know each other if you'd like," Crispin baited her and waited for a response, concerned about her sudden need to get to know him better. He wondered if Sister Lori had said something about him.

"Sounds fun, but I think we should spend a little more time here in town first before I go running off with you to some strange exotic place. Don't you even want to meet my parents first?" Diana giggled, blushing at the thought.

"Uh-huh, deal. I guess we're going to be having a lot more dates, huh? Sure, I want to meet your parents, Diana. I realize how important they are to you," Crispin replied.

"Yeah, we should hit the theatre soon; there's a bunch of new movies being released next week, but let's just take a nap so I can get ready to go to work, okay? My smashed car window already caused me to miss my training with Jackie today and I forgot to call so I'll still have to pay for taking up her time slot" she asked sweetly.

There was a knock on the door. It was Jessie.

"Hey, Di! I don't mean to disturb you, but Licorice just called me and told me that the club isn't going to be open tonight!" she yelled through the door. Diana thanked Jessie for the heads up and then she and Crispin fell fast asleep cuddled together happily.

"That sounds like good news to me, baby. Now we can snuggle and screw as long as we want, right?"

Diana rolled back over to face Crispin and gently chided him about blowing off the entire rest of the day. "Crispin, I've enjoyed every minute with you. But I need you to leave me alone for a bit so I can have a serious talk with my roommate about her recent inability to cover her share of the mortgage. Her boyfriend, Chad, is totally loaded, but I think he's getting bored supporting her coke habit and her rent. She's so stupid sometimes. I may have to kick her out tonight, and I don't want you to be here while I'm talking to her, understand?" Besides, if he didn't leave, how was she supposed to do some research on him? He was just so damned delicious; she didn't want to believe he was an evil person.

"Uh, yeah. Right," he said. "But I get to fornicate with my girlfriend one last time before we hook up again, right? I want to be sure you're still in a good mood of course."

Crispin smiled at her mischievously and began to rub his boxers again, having every intention of deluging Diana with lust so he could better seduce her. She seemed to be a strong-willed lady, so Crispin decided he needed to move slowly with Diana. She wasn't as mentally easy as others he'd seduced, but certainly that would make it even better.

"Absolutely. Then maybe I won't go so hard on her. As long as I don't have to dance. I'm just still so tired. I want to just lie here, be naked, and be lazy, 'kay?" Diana quickly sat up and began to remove her T-shirt and bra.

Crispin wasn't far behind in getting undressed. He made it perfectly clear that he wanted to lick her from head to toe or vice-versa, whichever came first. Diana was so pleased to be with a man so good-looking, skilled between the sheets, who did not require her tutorials, and who made her orgasms triumphant, that she had to confess to herself that she was becoming addicted to him. But she needed to rein in her impulsivity and study up on this guy more just in case Sister Lori was right about him. Clearly, it would be better to know earlier than later. Part of her couldn't help thinking that this was why women enjoyed bad boys so much! Except that Crispin didn't really fit the definition of a 'bad boy". He had a stable job in a professional career, a lovely home, no apparent addiction to alcohol or drugs and no 'baby-mama drama'.

An hour later, truly exhausted, they both fell asleep. Diana daydreamed of her new addiction, Crispin, and imagined having wild, passionate sex outdoor in her Hummer. She couldn't help but reflect on what Sister Lori had mentioned earlier. Oh, but why, why, why? Couldn't there still be some good guys left in the world? Maybe Sister Lori was wrong. Diana would go to the library tomorrow and find out for herself. No need to squash a good thing for now. Besides, Crispin was just the shot in the arm she needed right in her current singledom. Life had been becoming very monotonous. Since sex was generally a stimulus for Diana she lay there quietly watching Crispin and smiling, as he gazed up at her periodically kissing the air she breathed. Crispin was beginning to enjoy her company as well and felt less comfortable about possessing her soul, which was completely against the grain of his nature. He could suddenly understand the powerful draw a human relationship could have on an evil spirit such as his own.

"God, where did you learn to be so damned good with sex, Crispin? You're an animal!" They both lay there nude and breathless as the light of dusk peeked through the window.

"You know, Di, I read a lot too." He chuckled lightly and then pecked her on her nose.

"Oh please, Crispin, like you got those skills reading books. I must be a real dummy if I believe that crap!" Diana poked him in his tight, well-toned abs and then tickled him.

"Puh-lease, can you say years of practice?"

"Okay, Crispin, now I truly have blown my whole afternoon! Granted, I had you to keep me company." She pretended to pout and appear disappointed. "At the very least, I could've got my laundry done."

She laid back in his arms again and snuggled him. Shortly thereafter the both fell asleep and Jessie dared not to interrupt them again. A few hours later, Diana sat up with alarm. "Oh shit. What time is it? Crispin, get up. We dozed off and forgot to wake back up," she said, concerned as she noticed it was already dusk outside her window. She knew it was time for the inevitable discussion with her roomie. She wasn't looking forward to it, delivering bad news had never been her strong suit.

"Sorry, babe. You really knocked me out today." He rolled over, gave her a sizzling hot smile, and slowly and softly kissed her lips. Then he slid out of her bed and began to get dressed. "Now look, don't go too hard on your roomie after I leave. I'm sure there's a good reason for her delinquency. Try not to judge her too harshly, okay?"

Then off he swaggered, leaving Diana standing there half naked at the foot of her bed, but she was silently content to be alone for a moment. Now not only could she confront her roomie, but she could also head over to the public library and snoop on Crispin before she headed off to work at a local club, probably Leggs where her roommate had gone. She begrudgingly threw her shirt back on and padded softly down the hallway to Jessie's door.

Knocking lightly, she asked, "Jessie, can we talk for a few minutes alone, please?" She heard the low mumble of Chad's voice and then Jessie's chattering.

"Yeah sure, Di. Be right out." Jessie's feet thumped to the floor. Suddenly, the door popped open, and Jessie stuck out her blotchy face. Her hair was a mess, and last night's eyeliner was smudged under her eyes. Obviously she and Chad had been at it again, not like she and Crispin hadn't. "Hey listen, Jessie," Diana began as Jessie plopped down on the sofa beside her, "I've been meaning to speak with you about our rental agreement. It appears to me that you've been having trouble making your rent lately."

"Oh shit, Di, I know I've been really crappy lately, I've been late the past few months. I'm sorry. Will you forgive me?" Jessie frowned yet looked sincere. "I've taken too much time off work lately. Been trying to avoid Destiny … I think she stole some money from me last month during that huge computer seminar that came to town. I confronted her about it because I realized I left my clutch in the dressing room when I went back to my customer's table, and she was the only one in there at the time. When I ran back to get it, I asked her if anybody else had come back, because my purse looked a few bills lighter. Well, you know she went all crazy on me and slapped me, yelling at me and telling me not to accuse her because I didn't see anything. The thing is I know she did it; she was the only one there. I can't keep asking Chad for money. I can tell he's getting tired of it. I wish I wasn't such a pussy because my fear of her is keeping me from my work." Jessie's eyes began to water as she reached over to hug Diana. She returned the hug loosely and casually, not wanting to allow herself to become emotional, though she did truly value Jessie's friendship and felt sad for her.

"I understand, Jessie, but I can't continue to carry all the bills on my own without some help. After all, I probably wouldn't have gotten this place for us. I mean, look, I had my dad put his signature on the line for us because he believed in us. So what I'm saying is, get back to work, even if it means facing Destiny, or else I'm going to have to evict you."

"No, Diana, please don't evict me! I'll be forced to move back in with my mother. You know she's an alcoholic! Oh my God. I thought we were friends!" Jessie stood, crying and flailing her arms around.

Just then Chad came ambling out of the bedroom, rubbing his scruffy chin and looking alarmed. "What's going on out here?" he yelled at the girls.

"It's Diana, Chad. She's throwing me out!" By this time Jessie was hysterical.

"No, no, don't put that on me, Jessie. I simply asked you to start carrying your share again!" Diana screamed back at her and shook her head violently. "I'm getting the hell out of here! You two figure it out! You went back on our agreement, and you want me to pity you? That's bullshit, Jessie, and you know it! Fuck it. I tried to have a calm, rational conversation with you, but I'm done…at least you know how I feel. I'm outta here!" Diana threw the couch pillow she was holding at Jessie, grabbed her keys from the kitchen key hook, pushed past Chad, and stormed out, seething at how quickly Jessie had spun the truth.

Chapter 10

Now it was time for a quick run by the library to investigate Crispin, since her chat with Jessie had not gone quite as smoothly as she would have liked. She hoped it would be a futile visit, because Sister Lori was not going to ruin this great chance with Crispin for her. She knew she was already falling for him, and it was very difficult to find someone decent in the business she was in, so she didn't want to be too quick to judge him.

She was proud of herself for scribbling down the name of the tribe of Crispin's once he had repeated it again: Nephilim.

"Hello, my name is Danielle. I'm one of the library assistants. Can I help you find something this evening?" The woman was a short, plump redhead with bubblegum-pink framed glasses. She was certainly not one to follow the latest fashion trends. She looked every bit a nerdy girl who hung out in the library in her spare time.

"Oh yeah, hi. I'm Diana, and I'm trying to research a paper on an ancient tribe from the Bible days, the Nephilim? I'm trying to write a paper for class on this particular subject," she lied. Is there some way I can get some more information while I'm here?" Diana spun around so quickly that she almost smacked Danielle in the face with her large bosom. She couldn't help but giggle.

Danielle was extremely efficient in locating all the information Diana needed to do her research. She also seemed quite interested in the subject Diana was researching as she raced around the library, trying to grab as much information as possible. Diana was initially overwhelmed, but she recovered quickly, found a quiet space, and began to dig into the information. She was quickly intrigued with the legends and myths surrounding the race of Nephilim, and there seemed to be a strong difference in opinion between many spiritualists and academics as to whether they existed or not. The Nephilim had apparently been the target of many heated discussions between both believers and nonbelievers. It was simply too tedious, confusing, and time consuming to read about much more. She figured she'd read some more later. The simple truth was that she cared for Crispin.

Before she knew it, she'd dozed off at the library computer while still logged on to the internet. Awaking with a start, she knew it was time to go home. On the way out, her phone vibrated. Of course, it was Crispin. She smiled when she saw his name pop up on the screen.

"Hey, baby cakes, what's happening with you right now?" His voice was silky smooth over the phone. "You never called me back to tell me how it went with your roommate. I hope you weren't too hard on her. She seems cool. Man, do I miss you right now; you got me so twisted up already." He waited warily for her response.

"OMG! Crispin, she totally freaked out on me, giving this sob story about this other bitch we work with who stole her money and how she was afraid to go back and work with her! Then I told her she was going to have to figure something out because otherwise I'd have to evict her. That's when she went totally bonkers and told her boyfriend, Chad, the guy you met, that I was throwing her out! This agreement was never intended to be a free ride, you know. *Ugh*, I'm so tired, it's crazy." Diana felt good being able to vent to Crispin, though she was tired now and just wanted to go home and sleep.

"Wow, sounds a bit messy. I miss you though. Can you come over and play with me? I've been lonely ever since I left you today. If you're tired, come over here and sleep with me. Where are you anyway?"

Damn, he sounded good, she thought. If she went there, at least she could avoid seeing Jessie again tonight and maybe squeeze some answers from Crispin, and most certainly miss another night of earning income. Actually, it might just be a doubleheader for her. Besides, it was difficult to resist his sultry voice cooing on the phone to her. It made her hot just listening to him.

"Yeah, me too. I'm actually just leaving the library." She blushed. "But it's not far from your place. If you really want me to swing by, I should warn you, I'm really tired. I don't think I have much energy to play because I've been over here for a little while trying to locate some places for Jessie to move to in case I do throw her out," she lied, hoping to throw Crispin off her trail. "Wow, that really sucks, Di, but don't you think she should be looking for her own place? I mean, you're a good friend to want to help her and all," Crispin muttered, already feeling a bit suspicious of Diana's excuse for being at the library.

"Yeah, probably so, thanks," she shrugged, grabbing some apartment catalogs in a stand in the exit foyer of the library, holding her cellphone with her shoulder while talking quietly to Crispin.

Chapter 11

After hanging up the phone and heading out to her Hummer, Diana packed away her newly borrowed books about the Nephilim clan into her bag. She had already learned quite a bit from her two hours of research in the library. It seemed as though the theory was that this tribe was some sort of demon-human hybrid and that many of them still existed in the world today, impersonating humans. This made Diana somewhat nervous, but she felt compelled to have a discussion with Crispin about it. She would go to his home and talk with him tonight to quell her uneasiness. Besides, she'd never felt in harm's way when they were together, quite the opposite actually; she felt very safe around him. He allowed her to feel very feminine.

She hopped into her Hummer and drove off to hook up with Crispin. Maybe he could provide her some personal insight. She would be thrilled to maybe get some answers, since Sister Lori's warning had been so foreboding. On the way to Crispin's house, she cranked up her stereo, trying to forget the drama with her roommate. Soon she had the killer sound system blasting through her truck. The bass was pumping as she bobbed her head and sang to the beat of Madonna's "Express Yourself."

Soon she arrived at Crispin's door. "Hey Crispin, how are you feeling?" Diana reached up to kiss him and wrap her arms around his neck, her bag of books slung over her shoulder.

He felt so warm and strong. She'd missed him as well, though it had only been a few hours.

"*Mmm*, I'm much better now that you showed up!" He laughed, giving her a hearty hug and kiss in return, again flashing his megawatt smile. "I like these little shorts you're wearing, sugar. They're short enough yet not too short. It doesn't take much to fantasize about you!" He laughed quietly and slapped her behind.

"Well, I wouldn't want you to think I was too easy! Besides, I think I show enough of my ass at work already," Diana teased back. She quickly dropped her bag on the floor next to the door as Crispin snatched her up off her feet, cradled her, and glided quickly down the hallway to his lovely bedroom suite.

"I don't know why I just can't keep my hands off you, Diana! I just want to spread you on a slice of toast and gobble you up!" Crispin laughed. Then he dropped her carefully onto his bed and began to quickly undress, showing off his well-defined muscles from years of athletics and his current personal training.

Diana was just about to tell him to stop so they could discuss what she'd learned at the library, but after briefly feasting her eyes on him, she thought better of it. *Screw it*, she thought. *We'll talk later.*

"Come here, you!" He grabbed her by her thighs and pulled her toward him.

He quickly spread her legs, diving down and beginning to lick and nibble her passionately, preparing her for his entry.

"Whoa, Crispin, let a girl catch her breath a minute." She giggled, enjoying every minute of his "taking control" attitude.

"Baby, you can take all the breaths you need," as he licked his lips looking up at her. "I've been waiting to see you all afternoon!" He was clearly enjoying himself, busily buried between her thighs.

Diana was definitely enjoying his skillful prowess. Then a familiar song popped into her mind: "If loving you is wrong, I don't want to be right." This guy was just what she needed right now, a tasty break from work and her screwball roommate.

Right before they both climaxed, Crispin let out a spectacular, throaty yell, throwing his head back and attempting to hide his black eyes from Diana. She was scared witless, but her orgasm was phenomenal. Before she knew it, she'd let out a scream, frightening Crispin as well. He fell onto her, weak and exhausted and with a wicked look in his eyes.

"I'm sorry I frightened you, babe," he began softly. "Being with you gives me insane pleasure, and that was how I expressed it, I guess."

She smiled and looked into his bright green eyes, still a bit shaken. "No, that's fine. It just freaked me out, that's all. But I should know, is that how you always sound when you climax? I don't recall you doing that last night," Diana spoke gently and stroked Crispin's cheek.

"No actually, I didn't, but tonight I just couldn't help myself. I felt like an animal or something!" Crispin flashed his bright, sexy smile again and pulled Diana close to snuggle.

"You know, I'm glad you said that. It brings me to the real reason I'm here." Diana looked worried.

"So I'm not the real reason you're here?" Crispin seemed hurt as he rolled off her.

"Of course you are, silly!" Diana lightly punched Crispin's arm and giggled. "The real reason I was at the library was to look up the Nephilim clan you were talking about, a lot; they sound like scary people."

Crispin scratched his head and looked concerned. "I don't want to talk about this in bed. Let's go back out to the living room, not that we were ever there. I'll grab us some wine." He smiled nervously. Well, the inevitable moment he had known was coming had arrived. He frowned and slowly stood up.

Suddenly Diana's stomach was in knots because she couldn't tell if Crispin was upset or not. He didn't appear so, but then again she was still learning about him. Perhaps she shouldn't have brought it up, but she needed answers. Wrapped in his robe, Crispin gently took Diana's hand, offered her his other robe, and they strolled out to the great room. He motioned her to the sofa and then went to get a bottle of wine from the cooler in the kitchen. He came back with two glasses and then offered her one. She gladly accepted the glass, and he poured her some wine.

"Well shit, Diana. Why didn't you just ask *me*?" Crispin shook his head in confusion. "I would have been glad to tell you what I've learned about the Nephilim tribe; I know it appears as if its overtaken my life."

He poured himself some wine and lay back onto the sofa. He looked over at Diana quizzically. At this point, he figured he would just spit it out; she seemed interested enough to research him anyway, and she didn't seem to be terribly self-righteous or prejudging.

"Please don't be upset with me, Crispin. I just thought you didn't want to talk about it, that's all. And I was still curious because I really like you already." Diana batted her long lashes at him and pouted. "It sounded kind of creepy, the parts about fallen angels mating with human women and whatnot. I mean, isn't a fallen angel a demon or something?" Diana sipped her wine and eagerly waited for Crispin's explanation with wide eyes. She watched Crispin grin and stroke her exposed thigh. She reveled in the sensation of his skin against hers and listened attentively.

"Okay, Diana, here's the gist of it. Technically, I am a demon… Now, obviously, this is not something I generally tell people about myself, but I have a really good feeling about you. You're different than most human women I've been in contact with, and I seem to trust you already." Crispin sipped more wine and began to smile greedily at her again.

"What do you mean most human women, Crispin?" Diana appeared confused but still flushed from her recent liaison with her new boyfriend. He was simply delicious.

"I have fallen because I chose not to believe in a one true God, and where I'm from that's a really big deal, and it's a punishable offense in heaven. That's why I choose to just serve myself. I don't want to worship any one great entity. I just want to be happy and live my life. The problem is if you don't serve God, then by definition you serve Lucifer, and I don't want to believe that. I feel like I can't win here because I really don't want to serve either one. I hope you don't choose to think less of me because of who I am. My father always taught me to treat people right even though I am considered wicked by those who know of me. But if you decide you want nothing else to do with me, I can't make you stay. That's the power of free will, Diana. Wow. That's very refreshing. That's as honest as I've been in a long, long time with anyone. It actually felt pretty good. See, you're already having a good influence on me." He laughed and began to nuzzle her neck.

"Wow, Crispin, that's really deep shit you just laid on me there. I'm flattered by your honesty, but I don't know what else to say about this. It's so out of my league of understanding. I guess I thought if I asked you about it I would understand it better, but now I'm just more confused. It's all just so crazy. I'm sincerely baffled. But I don't really care as long as it doesn't affect my life." Diana shook her head slowly and then rubbed her tired eyes. "I'm too tired to process this. I'll think about it later maybe." She yawned. "I'm definitely ready for sleep now."

"All you really have to say is that you're willing to give me a chance to care for you, without passing judgment on me like Sister What's Her Face did."

Diana nodded. He pulled her close and squeezed her, feeling her relax and melt in his arms.

"Come on, baby. Let's go back to bed and sleep now, okay?" he gently asked her and carried her back to his bedroom.

"You know, Crispin, I don't judge you. I'm not in a position where I even feel comfortable with that," Diana mumbled into his chest. "Maybe someday you'll give me a reason to be frightened of you, but I'm a big girl and smart, so I'll make my own decisions. Right now I decide to spend the night with you."

They smiled at one another then fell into bed and soon dozed off together.

The following morning Diana awoke to the smell of bacon and eggs from the kitchen. Apparently Crispin had gotten up earlier and began making breakfast. It sure smelled good, and it was nice to have a real breakfast for a change instead of her typical fruit and protein shake.

She got up slowly and ambled out to the kitchen, bed head and all, in one of Crispin's old T-shirts. She walked up behind him and gave him a big squeeze.

"*Mmm*, yum" she said, "*you make breakfast too!*"

He turned around to face her, smiling. "Of course, baby, anything for you." He squeezed her back until some hot grease from the bacon popped out of the pan and burned his back, making him quickly pull away from the stove, laughing. "Ouch, shit!" he shouted as he bent down and smothered her with kisses.

"No, wait! I've still got morning breath! Not even coffee breath yet!" Diana exclaimed, laughing and covering her mouth.

"Let's sit and have a bite. Do you have time? I know you do your personal training in the morning," he said calmly as they sat at his glass-top dinette table.

Diana glanced up at the kitchen clock. "Yeah, I have time for a quick bite. At least an hour, but remember I still need to run home and get my clothes and bag." She winked at him and pulled her chair around the table to sit next to him so that their knees touched.

"Hey, Di, I realize that what I told you last night probably really freaked you out. I'm a bit surprised that you even stayed, though I'm happy you did. I'm really sorry about that. You caught me off guard because I really don't want to hurt you. We Nephilim have been given a bad rap, deservedly so I expect. Most people have no knowledge of our existence and the ones that do haven't painted us in a friendly light. But I'm different because my father raised me to be so. Sure, I still retain some supernatural abilities, that I use sparingly. But, more importantly, I don't use them to hurt people, especially people like you whom I've grown rather attached to. I'm very pleased that you decided to stay with me last night. It made me feel better about being honest with you. Quite frankly, I expected you to go running and screaming into the night." Crispin chuckled lightly, and then he turned somber.

"No doubt, Crispin, I certainly wasn't expecting you to come out with a confession to me, it was a bit overwhelming, but manageable. I mean, I did come here seeking answers, so I shouldn't be shocked, but I guess I was secretly hoping you would deny my research. I'm not thrilled you're a demon-angel-whatever. But I have to be honest with you; I'm having a very difficult time not being attracted to you. Of course, this explains the bullets bouncing off your chest and all, which you quickly explained away, but I suppose I have plenty to think about, huh? Where do we go from here?" Crispin quickly delivered their plates to the table while maintaining their conversation. Diana quickly gulped down her delicious breakfast, winked at him to demonstrate her approval and thanks.

Diana reached across the table and stroked Crispin's hand. "So far, I haven't felt fearful around you or anything. That could change, certainly. I don't know. I suppose we'll have to wait and see. But right now I need to run home for my clothes and shove off to my appointment. We'll have plenty of time to talk later, okay?" With that Diana planted a quick peck on Crispin's cheek and headed back to the bedroom to quickly dress and grab her bag.

As she drove home in the cool arid morning air of Vegas, she thought about how wonderful a person Crispin was and what he had told her about himself. How was she going to deal with this? She had finally met a really great guy, and he turned out to be a demon. Great! Some luck. Maybe she should seek spiritual counseling. But, not yet. As she pulled into her parking space at home, she didn't see Jessie's car. Maybe she stayed at Chad's last night, Diana figured. She jogged up to the door of the condo, unlocked it, and swung it open to find emptiness. She pulled a note from the refrigerator, which read,

> Dear Di,
>
> You've been a great friend, but I'm going to quit dancing now. It's really not for me anymore, which means I won't be able to afford to live with you now. I'm sorry about this. I'll probably work at my parents' Laundromat for a while until I can finish school. Chad and I are going to live together for a while until I can afford my own place. Please try to understand. I hope everything turns out with your new boyfriend, Crispin. He seems really cool and cute too! Call me whenever you want to talk.
>
> Love you much,
> Jessie

She had left her key taped to the fridge too. Well, that certainly wasn't what Diana had expected to come home to. But a quick look around the place gave evidence that Jessie had moved out. Everything except her bed was gone. She and Chad must have packed last night after Diana had stormed out. It was one more thing to think about, but she didn't want to keep Jackie waiting at the gym, so she grabbed her workout clothes and gym bag and rushed out the door. She was sad for both Jessie and herself. She popped in some Sarah McLachlan *Angel* and sped off to the gym

She was sad for both Jessie and herself. She popped in some Sarah McLachlan *Angel* and sped off to the gym.

Chapter 12

Diana wasn't really in the mood to work out today because she was stressed by her new boyfriend, Crispin, and grieving the loss of her roomie, Jessie. But she knew if she just got dressed and saw Jackie, she would probably get her mood back. Unfortunately, Jackie wasn't working today; she had called in sick and referred her clients to her friend/partner Dante, who was a handsome black man who clearly took his physique quite seriously.

"Hi, I'm Diana," she said bravely, extending her hand for a shake.

"Oh yeah, my name is Dante. I'm your trainer. Jackie asked me to train for her today because she's not feeling too well," he replied, shaking her hand.

He had big brown eyes that reminded Diana of a lost puppy. There was a hint of Dolvett, the baldhead black trainer on the Biggest Loser. But his biceps and thighs didn't look lost in the least. Diana told Dante that she and Jackie usually began with some cardio to warm up, so she hit the treadmill for a short five-minute run and then went right back to his side. Apparently Jackie had left specific instructions for their workout today.

"Wow, Diana," he began when she jogged back to him. "I'm surprised you even need a trainer, because you're the hottest client I've ever trained." Eyeballing her, he chortled into his fist and tried not to be seen checking out her large breasts.

"Thanks, Dante. Actually, I'm a dancer over at Olympia Garden, so I get quite a workout at my job. But honestly I just don't always think it's enough, you know? I mean, I don't want to get lazy when I quit dancing because I forgot what the inside of a gym looks like, you know? My boyfriend is a bit of a gym junkie too. He works out across town at Gold's."

"*The* Olympia Garden, huh?" Dante nodded in approval. "That's a real nice club they got over there. Yeah, my homies took me over there for my birthday last year. They've got some beautiful ladies, I recall. Anyway, you've gone and gotten me all distracted and everything; let's get down to your workout because *my* time is *your* money, as they say!" He snickered. Dante had a light, easygoing personality that didn't immediately pair up with his large physique, but he was affable and friendly and made his clients feel comfortable in his presence. Diana couldn't help but wonder if the rumor that big guys had small packages was true.

"Well anyway, I'm glad to hear you enjoyed our club. But gravity sucks, as they say, and I can't do it forever!" Diana punched Dante jokingly in his large, muscular arm, and he smiled in agreement.

Dante deviated from Jackie's workout agenda on several of the exercises. On some things, he simply had a better technique; he'd been training much longer than Jackie and had a whole lot of the gym's customers as his personal clients. Diana was grateful to change up her routine a little, but she knew she'd be sore tomorrow.

As she left the gym, she waved at Dante and thanked him for subbing for Jackie, though she knew Jackie would be taking a percentage. She was just happy to be heading home, but then the looming thought of Jessie leaving kicked her in the gut. Suddenly, she was sad again. She had been distracted by Dante and her workout for the past hour. Now she would be heading home to an empty house. Even though Jessie's boyfriend was annoying, being the cokehead that he was, it was still cool coming home to some noise occasionally.

Diana was not afraid to live alone, but the primary issue was going to be covering the monthly payments alone, because clearly when her father cosigned for the condo, it had been based on the incomes of both ladies, not Diana's alone. Though Diana was capable of making the payment alone, it would severely sidetrack her financial plans for the future, as she was saving a large part of her earnings in an IRA, because she knew dancing wasn't going to be a long-term career choice. And she ultimately still wanted to attend law school without her daddy helping all the way.

When she finally arrived home, she was exhausted and achy after her workout with Dante, so she dropped her bag at the door and collapsed on her bed, thinking about the past few days with Crispin. As time went on (several weeks, now) Diana and Crispin continued to see each other, though Crispin had become less interested in dropping by her place of work. So far he seemed to working out great in the boyfriend role, he hadn't freaked out about her being a dancer yet. But the constant thought of him being a demon was really beginning to gnaw at her. She kept pushing the thought to the back of her mind, but whenever she caught his eyes turning black, it always sent a chill up her spine. But she was never frightened to go to dinner with him or even stay over at his house. He'd always made sure she was welcome and comfortable around him and his house.

Crispin was attentive, generous, sensitive, charming, and a true devil in bed. She was beginning to think she was really falling in love with him, but she needed more time to think about it; after all, the business had taught her that men were a dime a dozen, even the ones who seemed cool at first like Crispin.

After meeting with Sister Lori, occasionally, who continued to warn her to dump him (with little or no evidence), one afternoon for lunch, she felt a need to hold on tighter. The fact that he didn't stress her about quitting her job made him especially sexy.

So far Diana had been able to avoid Crispin meeting her parents, though it was harder to keep him from her father, who was out and about more, and Crispin had been staying over at her place more often since Jessie had moved out. It was less lonely and creepy there when Crispin stayed over; he always made Diana feel safe. Though, she generally preferred his home to hers.

Chapter 13

A few weeks later, Crispin rolled into the local 7-Eleven on his lunch break, he noticed the same three guys outside that he recalled seeing at the club the night Diana's vehicle had been vandalized and the club robbed. He sat patiently in his vehicle for fifteen minutes, watching them talk on their cell phones and slurp their Big Gulps, and then he heard his demon voice begin to whisper to him. "*Those are the guys. Kill them,*" it hissed. Quickly Crispin went into autopilot and his demon nature overtook him.

The police had been unable to follow up with Diana on the whereabouts of the suspects who damaged her vehicle and had ultimately dropped the investigation. But Crispin needed closure, so as another vehicle entered the parking lot in front of them, he glared over at the driver, causing the car to shoot full speed ahead, driving right into the young men and smashing them through the glass window of the store.

People screamed and ran out of the store. Eventually someone helped the driver from her vehicle; she appeared to be unharmed, but she was confused. Crispin got out of his car and strolled casually and invisibly into the store to check his work, aware that the security cameras were wide awake. The three guys lay on the floor or pinned against the supplies rack. They were bloody. Satisfied that he'd avenged Diana's vandalism and hearing sirens in the distance, he walked over to the cooler and stole a Pepsi for himself while everyone else was preoccupied with the emergency at hand. Crispin hurried out of the store then jumped into his Corvette. As he sped away, he could hear the ambulances in the distance.

"Hey, baby," he chirped after dialing Diana's phone as though nothing had happened. "Whatcha doing?"

"Well, I was just going to head over to Chad and Jessie's place to check in on them. I haven't seen her in over a week. She looked a bit peaked last time and said she and Chad were having trouble adjusting to living together."

"Yuck, that's a real bummer, but I must admit he didn't strike me as the loyal type. And if you're living with a lady, I'd imagine that would really hamper your hounding around because now you're accountable for your comings and goings, not to mention any mysterious phone calls. Damn, that was a recipe for disaster." Crispin sounded concerned, but he was secretly happy that he'd exacted revenge on Diana's suspects and nobody knew but him.

Well, maybe that was why nobody lived with Crispin, Diana thought. Perhaps he had commitment issues too and just hid them, trying to keep his secret safe.

"Well, actually," Diana began, "I think it was Chad who suggested that she stay with him. Maybe it was just pity. I don't know. What are you up to today other than working?" Diana figured it would be safer and less awkward to change the subject.

"Well, I'm still out on lunch. I have some flexibility, so I was thinking about swinging by and picking you up. You always make such a terrific lunch date. What do you think?" Crispin sounded so sweet and delectable, but she needed to stay focused on her friend.

"That sounds fun Crispin, but Jessie really needs me right now. Come by my house later before I leave for work, okay?" With that, she pressed the *End* button and ran out the door.

Crispin was beginning to feel like Diana was more interested in Jessie's welfare lately than his own needs. Jealousy was not a color he wore well. But he was certain Jessie didn't need to continue to be a factor in their relationship much longer. There was no way she could compete with his love for her. He still had time to work it all out. No hurry. He headed back to the office, sipping away on his drink. On the radio, he heard a this-just-in announcement about the sudden accident at the 7-Eleven, and he grinned menacingly to himself. Apparently the driver of the vehicle had been under the influence, coincidentally, so crashing through the store made perfect sense, Crispin thought.

When Diana approached the door of Chad's apartment, she hesitated before she rang the bell, feeling slightly uneasy that she'd even come. *Ding-dong.* The door whisked open right away. It was Chad standing there, half dressed, holding a pillow over his privates.

"Hey, Diana. What's up with you today?" Chad smiled, looking slightly awkward and embarrassed. "I didn't expect to see you anytime soon! Sorry, I don't normally answer the door like this, but I was kinda busy. But what can I help you with? I hope you're not here looking for Jessie, 'cause she moved out already."

He grinned again and tried to appear sorry as a naked redhead girl bustled behind him past the door. "I think she moved back home with her mom. It wasn't really working out, you know?" He took no mind of the girl running around anxiously behind him, trying to locate her clothing.

Diana spied her through the crack in the door where Chad's head was peeking out.

"Yeah, she mentioned briefly that you guys were having a hard time, but does she also know that you're fucking around on her too?" Diana gave Chad a searing look of disapproval.

She started to walk away, but he grabbed her arm and stopped her. "Look, Diana, we already broke up, so there's no reason for you to be coming around here anymore! Who I fuck is none of your damned business! Excuse me." He slammed the door, and she quickly split the premises.

She wondered why Jessie hadn't mentioned that she and Chad were broken up. Maybe she was too embarrassed. Diana figured she'd just try calling her over at her mother's later on. She needed to head home and get ready for work anyway.

Work that night was exhausting for Diana; it seemed that ever since the club made the news because of the burglary, every guy in town, visitors as well, wanted to get over there. Many nights it was literally standing room only, with barely any room for the dancers to move around. After working all night, Diana couldn't wait to go home and fall into Crispin's arms after taking a short shower to wash the smoke and dust from her body and hair. If he wasn't at his home, he was always sitting up, at her apartment waiting to greet her no matter how late or early, since Vegas clubs were open twenty-four hours with girls working three eight-hour shifts around the clock. Diana was scheduled for the 9pm to 5am shift. It was often very early when she arrived home or at Crispin's

This was one of those days, but Crispin embraced her and gladly ran her a bath and headed out to the kitchen to make her some tea. She'd been spending more and more nights at Crispin's house; it was less lonely, and he was very comforting. Besides, Crispin had a fabulous flat-screen television mounted above his bathtub. He said a person should be able to soak and relax while watching his or her favorite shows.

As Diana climbed into the bubbly tub, Crispin came in with hot tea—pomegranate, her favorite flavor—for Diana and a bottle of wine for himself. Diana slid down into the tub and began to tell Crispin about her day, first at Chad's apartment and then at work. Crispin nodded calmly as he listened. Then he pointed at the TV, where the news anchor was reporting the incident at the 7-Eleven earlier that day. Diana was totally shocked as she saw the faces of the victims flashed up on the screen. Crispin giggled, and she chided him.

"What the hell is so funny, Crispin?" She splashed some water at him.

"Well, I know you don't recognize them, but those are the same guys who smashed up your car window. You know what they say: what goes around comes around. The cops couldn't find them, but they got caught anyway! Hell, better yet, they got dead anyway!" Crispin could barely contain himself, knowing that he had everything to do with it.

"Crispin, two of the guys are dead from the accident, and one guy's in critical condition. I don't think they deserved that, do you?" Diana was turned off by his insensitivity. "Yeah, I was pissed off that they

Bright Lights and Promises

busted my window, but it's fixed now. It doesn't matter anymore. God, I can't believe you sometimes! I'm going to bed now. I think you're drunk or something. Hand me my towel please. This bath is so over, thank you."

She climbed out of the bathtub, but Crispin tossed her over his shoulder, took her into the bedroom, and began to lick her from toe to head. He was already in the groove when Diana tried to pull her wet hair from beneath her and out of her towel. She had barely caught her breath before his naked body was on top of her, consuming her completely.

"I'm not so drunk after all, am I?" he joked as he lost himself in her.

An hour later, Diana pleaded to just sleep, and Crispin was happy to comply and cuddle. He gloated in his sleep that he had exacted revenge on two of the punks who had hurt Diana. He had begun to notice that his demon was becoming more defensive of Diana and less likely to want to destroy her. But there was still war within him. He was beginning to fall in love in a very human way with her, which had not initially been the plan. He knew it would be dangerous for him and for her as well, because his inner demon were extremely destructive. If only his father were still around to guide him, though his father had found himself in the same predicament with Crispin's mother. For now he would just snuggle her and not worry himself.

"Crispin, wake up. You're talking in your sleep, and it's really creepy." Diana rolled over and gently shook him awake.

He slowly opened his eyes, and at that very moment he knew he loved her. "Huh? What's wrong, Di?" He squinted at her.

"You were saying, 'Just kill them. Kill them.' It really frightened me. Were you dreaming or something?" Diana was puzzled yet groggy.

"Oh yeah, baby. I was having a dumb nightmare again. I'm so sorry I woke you. I was watching *Transformers* while I was up waiting for you because I knew an action movie would keep me awake. I was probably yelling at the TV again. I hope you can go back to sleep." He held her close and was glad he had covered for himself so quickly.

Chapter 14

Morning always came too soon for Diana, especially since she didn't get off work until five in the morning, but without fail Crispin always managed to get up at 6:00 a.m. so he could shower and make coffee and still get to work by 8:00 a.m.

He always gave Diana a kiss good-bye, but this time when he kissed her, he whispered, "I love you," in her ear.

She smiled softly and sleepily rolled over to hug his pillow and return to sleep. She didn't typically rise before noon, so sleep was still her best friend. When Diana awoke around eleven thirty, she figured she'd give Jessie a call from Crispin's.

Jessie answered on the second ring. "Hello? This is Jess."

"Hey, girlfriend. Wassup? It's Diana! I'm so glad you're okay! I haven't talked to you in like forever!"

"Hey, Di. What's up? I mean, we did see each other a week ago over at Chad's place, remember?" Jessie sounded somber and distant.

"I know, but I got used to seeing you every day, so it's weird when I don't know what's going on every minute of your life, you know? I miss you so much; I know I have Crispin, but he's not a girl or a dancer, so I don't feel comfortable sharing everything with him." Diana tried to maintain her enthusiasm, but she could feel nothing from Jessie on the other end of the line, so she decided to take a more somber approach. "Um, is everything going okay with you and Chad right now?"

Finally she got a response at the mere mention of Chad's name. "No,

Di. As a matter of fact, I broke up with that son of a bitch!" Jessie's voice shifted to a tone of irritation and disgust. "I came home from work early one afternoon, and some redheaded bitch went running half naked from our apartment." Jessie began to sob. "That bastard! I knew he was up to something when I was working! But he always lied about it! I packed my shit that afternoon and told him good-bye forever! I don't give a damn what he does now! Asshole."

Diana didn't want to be the one to say *I told you so*, so she didn't. They both had known that Chad was a good-for-nothing sleazebag, even though he believed he was the hottest thing since sliced bread. Yeah sure, he had money and good looks, but that's what made him such a jerk. His rich daddy in Lebanon was always fronting him money for managing their local gas station, which he managed to check in on about three days per week, and the rest of the time he was chasing after strippers, who were all too ready to help him unload some of his cash. He tolerated this behavior for about three months with each girl; Jessie was his latest victim, unfortunately for her.

"Wow, Jessie. I'm really sorry! That's so shitty," Diana replied, wanting to hug her, but also recalling seeing a naked redhead scurrying around Chad's apartment when she went for a visit.

"Yeah, I know, but I see from the caller ID that you're calling from Crispin's house. So I suppose things are still going good with him, huh?" Jessie was secretly envious but happy for Diana all the same.

"Uh-huh, so far so good. I think I'm beginning to really fall in love with him. That's scary for me, you know? I don't know if I feel comfortable letting my guard down. It's weird because I haven't been with somebody in so long and I've had this wall up or something." Diana felt comfortable talking to Jessie about these things. "He's always so concerned about me and wants to protect me, but I don't know if it's because he's—" She stopped midsentence, recalling that she had not told Jessie about Crispin being a demon.

"Because he's what, Diana?" Jessie jumped on the hanging statement.

"Never mind. I was gonna say an accountant type who's always worrying about people's funds. I think it makes him worried a lot, sometimes obsessive. That's all." Diana sighed with relief that she had blocked Jessie's inquiry. It would have been really be great if Jessie was less hostile right now so Diana could truly confide in her like the good old days. Oh how she desperately wished she had a close friend to talk to these days, one who didn't have some grudge or ulterior motive. She would just have to work this one out on her own.

Chapter 15

Across town, Crispin was at work, secretly manipulating stocks in his clients' favor so he could continue to stay profitable and eventually gain management over the department by showing increased dividends for the firm. He didn't particularly care for the manager, David Helms; he was a bit too timid, Crispin thought, and the fact that he was fifty pounds overweight, it couldn't be very good for his health. He was always breathing heavily and drinking too much coffee.

Maybe he should just have a heart attack, Crispin devised to himself. Nobody would really miss him. He had no family, and Crispin was next in line for the boss's position. Then he would earn a handsome salary plus commission, and he could afford for Diana to quit her job (secretly he did find her job disturbing as he regularly recalled the dance she'd given him) and move in with him so he could take care of her. He was getting ahead of himself, he knew, but Diana had really pierced his heart. She made it hard for him to be a demon sometimes. *Perhaps love does that*, he thought. Just as Crispin was daydreaming in his leather chair, watching the trading ticker dance across his computer screen, Carl Watts, another broker, came busting into his office.

"Crispin, man, holy shit! You're not gonna believe what just happened!"

"Holy hell, Carl. What's going on? What's happening? Why are you so freaked out?"

Crispin was cool and collected, but Carl was having an all-out hissy fit as he dragged Crispin from his desk to look out the window. An ambulance was waiting at the front doors of the firm. Crispin was now truly concerned.

"Look, man! David just fell over at his desk this afternoon. They're wheeling him out right now, man! Some of the guys were saying he was on hypertension meds; he'd been trying to lose weight, but he was having a hard time. He may have had a heart attack. I think he might be dead. Wow! Crispin, that would totally suck for his wife if he did."

Crispin looked surprised. "Oh, you didn't know he was married? But I guess you know you're next in line for his position because of your seniority ... uh, sorry. I guess that was pretty insensitive of me, huh?"

Carl seemed exasperated and looked to Crispin for some sort of emotion, but Crispin only shook his head and walked away, speechless, quietly sneering even he knew it would be rude to rejoice at a promotion caused by his boss dying. But being of a malevolent nature, he found it impossible to grieve. He couldn't believe that David's obese body had beaten him to the punch, but he was quietly thrilled all the same. If David did in fact die, Crispin would really have to step it up to fill his shoes as new management.

No problem, he thought. Fate worked in even his favor once in a while, maybe. But it wouldn't hurt to swing by the hospital later on after work to check on the third guy who'd busted Diana's car window, he mused, and perhaps even David. Right then his phone pinged; it was a text from Diana. It simply read, *I love you too.* Crispin smiled at his phone warmly and was surprised she'd heard him this morning when he'd left. She had barely acknowledged him leaving.

He'd make it a point to take her out to dinner tonight so they could speak to each other without being distracted by the bedroom. He knew she'd appreciate that. There wasn't much else to do at the office now that the boss was being wheeled away. Hell, maybe they could all check out early today.

On his drive home, Crispin called P.F. Chang's, one of their favorite local restaurants, and made a five o'clock reservation for him and Diana. Then he phoned her, and she agreed he could pick her up for dinner before her shift began. Of course, Crispin was thrilled to be having dinner out with his favorite girl. Though he had become quite accustomed to cooking for them, eating out would be a nice change.

Once he was home, he grabbed himself a bottled water from the fridge and figured he had enough time to run by the hospital and check on the third guy, who was still in critical condition, and look in on his boss too. When Crispin arrived at Sunrise Hospital, he parked and quickly headed upstairs, avoiding the cameras in the back stairwell. When he reached the nurses' station, he asked a nurse what room Robby Hanson was in (His inner demon had already made him aware of the boy's name). She directed him down the hallway to room 378. Crispin's evil nature made him want to leap with joy that he was able to get to him, but he remained cool as usual.

As he strolled down the bleak pale green hallway to room 378, he saw that a young nurse was just leaving the room, but she couldn't help but flirt and bat her eyelashes at him. Crispin was used to having this effect on ladies. He didn't mind or even care to notice anymore.

Robby was clearly in bad shape, but he looked hopeful as he turned to meet Crispin's gaze. The machines made their typical bleeping sounds as Crispin slowly approached his bedside. Immediately his eyes changed to black as he grinned deviously at Robby.

"Whoa, dude. Who the hell are you?" Robby shrank back in fear and confusion.

"I'm your worst fucking nightmare, dude." Crispin laughed evilly. "You don't have the right to live, asshole, after what you did to my girlfriend!" he spoke emphatically under his breath.

With that, he glanced up at the heart monitor and flat lined it. Robby took one last breath and then died. Sirens rang throughout the floor, and nurses scrambled to rush a crash cart to Robby's room. Crispin immediately became invisible and slipped out through the back stairwell. Once he made it to his car, he was visible again and smiled snidely at his handiwork. He felt it was unfortunate that he hadn't had a chance to swing by his boss's David's room as well, to confirm his untimely death.

Chapter 16

Diana waited patiently at home for Crispin to pick her up for their dinner date before she went to work. As usual, he was punctual, and she was casually sexy. They hugged each other tightly and kissed passionately. Then Crispin picked up her bag for work, and they headed out the door. Always a gentleman, he opened Diana's door, and she slid into his bucket seat, exposing just enough thigh from underneath her purple mini-dress to seduce Crispin's always active imagination. He was really only looking forward to sitting with Diana and discussing the nature of their relationship, but if that should lead to something else, he would welcome that as well.

At dinner, Crispin could not take his eyes off of Diana, and she couldn't take her eyes off him either. They both grinned coyly at one another.

"You know," he began, "I was certain I wouldn't find anyone to love in my lifetime like my father did. My mother was the center of his world, and she was also a very beautiful human woman." Crispin shifted slightly in his seat to move in closer to Diana.

She grinned at him. "So was your mother also a stripper, Crispin?" She was embarrassed to ask but felt it was fair to know. Maybe exotic dancers were an Achilles heel for Nephilim men.

"Uh, no. Actually, my mother was a server at the fancy Bellagio casino/restaurant here. I have forgotten how exactly the met by now, but I'm glad they did." Crispin smiled gingerly at her.

"Okay, that's good to know. One less thing for me to worry about. But speaking of restaurants, it was really nice to come out to eat with you and not always have you slaving away in the kitchen, though you know how much I enjoy your cooking. This way we can sit together and look lovingly into each other's eyes. No hustle and bustle. Just you and me, baby. I take it you got my text, earlier. Does that have anything to do with why you're taking me out tonight?" Diana teasingly pinched his cheek.

"Yes, baby. I smiled when you told me that you loved me too, and I was shocked because I didn't even think you heard me when I left this morning. But I need to be honest with you about something, Diana. I mean, I don't have to, but I want to. Obviously you already know about my history as a Nephilim and the implications of that, but I find myself in a conundrum with you because I've fallen in love with you and I wasn't supposed to. I thought I could control it, but the more I get to know you, it's becoming much harder to do. I'm supposed to want to harm you, to possess your soul. But I can't. I … I just want to protect you. It really scares me."

"Wait a minute, Crispin. I've fallen for you too, but are you saying that in the beginning, I was just a victim to you? Boy, what a big dummy I was. I'm so hurt to hear you say this! I find this really hard to believe. You've never given me any reason to fear you except the day your eyes got all black when you met Sister Lori at my condo. That was a bit freaky. She warned me about you and told me you were an evil person and not to be trusted. At first I thought she might just be jealous because you are so hot and she's not supposed to have lusty thoughts about men. But even though she's a nun, she'd have to be blind not to notice how incredibly delicious you are. Anyway, I couldn't pull away from you, even when I found out your creepy secret about being half human and half demon. I've always felt safe with you, ever since you rescued me from that nightmare at the club that night. You were my knight in shining armor. Now you're telling me that you wanted to hurt me! So, what were you doing, just biding your time?"

Diana found herself getting loud and slowly standing up, but she quickly realized the purpose of having this discussion in a public place;

nobody liked an audience, though she did dance in front of an audience most nights. She quickly sat back down, regaining her composure. "Now I am actually frightened of you. You totally switched up on me," she hissed at him between clenched teeth. "I feel like we've spent so much time with each other, and I was considering going up to your cabin at Lake Tahoe. But wow. I don't think so now! The hairs on my arm are standing up. Now, I'm just so disappointed with you, Crispin. How dare you? You lied?" Finally Diana stopped and just stared at him. Her heart rate was elevated, and she put her hand on her chest to calm down.

"Are you done now?" Crispin looked bewildered. "I don't think you were really listening to me, Diana. I came here to declare my love to you, not to hurt you. That was my point tonight. I have begun to care so much about you that I only want to protect you and hurt the people who hurt you. Diana, the humanity in me has taken over. It really surprises me, that's all. I've never let this happen before. I wish my father was around to talk to me about this. I told you that my mother was a human woman too. This is why I live alone. To protect myself from feelings like this, but somehow you got underneath my skin. Please don't be angry with me. I feel like I'm just another regular guy who was caught off guard by love. I thought I was in control, but the past few months I've grown weaker and weaker. It's so crazy."

"Crispin, I've heard enough for tonight. Please just take me to my house. I need some time alone." Diana stood abruptly, tossing her cloth napkin on the table and leaving the remaining food on her plate. "Thanks for dinner and your bullshit conversation. I don't even know what to think now. This is not the conversation I wanted to have with you. I was actually considering introducing you to my folks now, since they've been asking to meet you. Ugh, never mind. Let's just go, please."

"Diana, wait. Don't leave me. Shit!" Crispin quickly jumped up from the table, grabbed her arms, looked squarely into her eyes, and professed his feelings once again. "Diana, I'm in love with you! Dammit, and I don't care who knows it. Do you want me to stand up on this table and yell it out to the entire restaurant? I will if it will make you believe me!"

At this point Crispin's voice had carried down the aisle, and a server ran over to them. "Is there a problem over here? I can get the manager if you need me to."

He shrank back when Crispin glared at him with black eyes and said, "Back off!"

The young server quickly scrambled away to his next table.

After paying the bill, Crispin quickly sped Diana back to her condo. She crossed her arms across her chest and didn't speak a word. She was seething with anger about Crispin. She could not believe she had let her guard down once again. But this time, she had really fallen hard.

When they finally made it to her condo, Diana leapt out of the Corvette, not waiting for Crispin to open the door. She rushed up to her door, with Crispin following quickly behind.

"Diana, I know you're pissed at me. I would be too if I were you. I was just hoping we could talk about this more, okay? I adore you, baby. Please don't do this," Crispin gently begged as Diana stormed into the condo, leaving the door hanging open for him.

"Crispin, what the hell do you expect me to say?" Diana turned toward him, looking flabbergasted and sad as she fell onto the sofa and habitually turned on the television. "From what I understand, you've wanted to harm me from the beginning, but for whatever reason you haven't, so instead you trick me into believing you're this fabulous guy or whatever? I mean, crap, I don't even know if you're telling me the truth. How do I know you're not trying to trick me now?" Crispin just looked at her and shook his head, knowing he could never reveal the truth about his revenge on the guys who damaged Diana's car, all of which he justified due to his love for her. It would simply devastate her to know the truth; clearly the conversation had taken a turn for the worse.

Diana collapsed more deeply into her sofa and threw her hands over her face, weeping. Crispin tried to sit next to her and hold her, "Please, just go, Crispin. Let me think alone for a while. It's just too much to process right now!" She waved him away, and he got up and left quietly. He felt awful about the mess he'd made, yet he was sure that he and

Diana were far from over. He was certain his evil nature could not come between their now professed love for one another. Besides, she had no idea that he was behind the murder of the three guys who had damaged her vehicle.

Diana slowly headed back to her bedroom, which she scarcely used anymore since she usually stayed with Crispin. She pulled off her dinner dress and tossed it on the floor. Then she threw on an old New York Giants sweatshirt an ex-boyfriend had given her to wear and fell onto her bed, exhausted but too tired to sleep. She decided to call in sick to work. *Nothing can make you feel queasier than a breakup*, she thought. A pint of Ben & Jerry's Cherry Garcia should be good enough to drown her sorrows tonight, she mused with a grin.

Chapter 17

Soon afterward she was bawling into her pillow, thinking about Crispin and how wonderful it had been the past few months. She tried to make herself think bad things about him so she could justify breaking up. But no matter how hard she tried, she couldn't think bad things about him. He hadn't made her quit her job. He never even seemed jealous about her work, though he didn't come in and hang out and distract her either. After Diana retrieved her ice cream from the freezer, she plopped back into her comfy bed and turned on the news as a distraction.

"Oh my God," she found herself speaking to the TV. "All those guys are dead now. I can't believe this." Diana choked back a few tears of sympathy for them, and then a strange thought occurred to her. Something Crispin had said during dinner about wanting to hurt people who tried to harm her. *I wonder*, she thought, *if he had anything to do with this. No way, that's offensive, I won't ask him that because I'm pretty certain that I don't want to know.*

What if he had? Could she still love him, knowing he had something to do with the untimely demise of these men? What if he killed her? Maybe she should go back to the library and study some more and read up on this guy. He was so wonderful, but knowledge was power.

She ran over to her desk, logged on to her always waiting laptop, and began to search every possible synonym for the words *Nephilim* and *demon*. One point became evident: demons couldn't die, so shooting one or hurling a cross at one wasn't going to kill it. *Well, this all makes* sense now, she thought. *No wonder Crispin wasn't hurt when he rescued me from the club that night, even though he said he was wearing protection.* She'd been such a fool. Oh well. There she sat, alone and pondering her world, when the phone rang, almost scaring the life out of her.

"Hello?" she asked, already having a keen idea who it was without glancing at the caller ID.

"Hi, sweetheart. I'm really sorry," said a calm, sad, yet cool voice from the other end. "I didn't take you out to dinner so that we could break up, you know? Trust me. I saw that going in a totally different direction. Can I just come back over now and stay with you? It feels awfully lonely here. I promise you, no more drama tonight, okay? I just don't want to be alone without you; I know somehow I screwed up, okay? Please forgive me."

"Well, the way I see it, we just survived our first real argument, huh?" Diana questioned back, not terribly eager to forgive him yet. "I'm lonely too, Crispin, but we stay here tonight just in case you get any ideas." She chuckled and hung up the phone.

Surely he would be willing to answer more questions about himself, she thought, even if she really didn't have much to ask tonight. She still enjoyed having her snuggle buddy around. The truth was evident, demon or not, Crispin was an exceptional boyfriend who she ultimately planned on introducing to her parents. She didn't feel stupid at all, that she'd let her guard down to feel again. He had definitely made it worthwhile.

Diana began to think that she should make a visit to her former Catholic high school and speak with one of her favorite teachers about all of this, or maybe even one of the priests, though there was always the threat of them passing judgment on her profession and her boyfriend, as well. She would see if anyone would be around after the weekend but would try to enjoy Crispin until then at least. No, on second thought, she wouldn't discuss Crispin with anyone except Sister Lori, who already knew his dark secret. She had promised him, keeping his secret safe was the least she could do for him saving her life.

Just then, her phone rang. It was Sister Lori.

"Hello, Diana. I'm sorry to call so late, but during my prayer session this evening the spirit led me to call you and tell you that demons cannot be trusted. Their sole mission is the destruction of your soul. They know all our human weaknesses and are all too happy to use them against us. They cannot tell the truth because it would be a direct violation of their demonic nature, so please, please be very cautious of your boyfriend, Crispin. Good-bye now and good luck. May God bless you." Diana never got a word in, in Crispin's defense. But didn't feel like dealing with Lori that night. She simply refused to call her back.

With that warning, Sister Lori quietly hung up the phone. Diana slumped in her bed, awaiting Crispin's arrival. She was too upset to move when the doorbell rang and frightened her out of her fog. She scrambled around her room, picking up a little, wondering what she'd say when she saw his face. Then she rushed to the door and swung it open to reveal Crispin standing there, breathtakingly handsome, with a bouquet of red roses and wine in his arms.

"Look baby, I'm sorry, okay? I messed up somehow. Please don't hate me. I couldn't bear it because I've already fallen in love with you." He handed the roses to her through the doorway and pulled her close to embrace her.

God, Diana thought, *he's so wonderful. But I need to keep my distance for a while,* she chided herself. "Come on in, Crispin. We clearly need to talk about us."

Diana sat cross-legged on the sofa next to him. She offered him a drink, but he refused.

"Uh, I don't really know how to ask this question, so I guess I'll just spit it out: did you have anything to do with those three guys dying, the ones who damaged my car?" She sat back, relieved, and waited for his answer; she couldn't help but to stare at his full, kissable lips. She was surprised that her mouth betrayed her thoughts, since she never intended to ask him that question.

Crispin stood slowly and said, "I think I'll have that beer now, Di." He strolled toward the fridge and grabbed a beer out of it. "Does it really matter?" he then asked her. "I mean, whether I did or didn't, it's pretty obvious to me that they got what they deserved, right?" He sat back down next to her and swigged his beer, watching her carefully.

"No, Crispin. They didn't get what they deserved! Except maybe the one guy who was on the most wanted list and had already raped two people. So did you or didn't you?" Diana was growing impatient. "No political answers, Crispin."

"Unfortunately, I didn't, baby, but I wish I had," he lied calmly. He then bent over her on the sofa and planted a firm kiss on her lips before falling back down onto the couch.

"*Whew!* That's good! Even better, that's great!" Diana relaxed a bit.

"What would make you even think something like that? Do you find me that sinister? Promise me you don't think that poorly of me, baby." Crispin suddenly appeared to have his feelings hurt.

"I don't know, Crispin. I'm sorry, that was rude. It's just that when you said you wanted to harm people who harmed me, I guess ..." Diana looked apologetic.

"Oh, Diana, I didn't mean that I wanted to kill people," Crispin pleaded, knowing exactly what he had meant. "I was only trying to express my heartfelt feelings for you, honey. I won't hurt anyone, okay? I promise." He seemed concerned with keeping his promise to her, although he was already on a revenge mission.

He sucked down the last gulp of his beer and wiped his mouth with the back of his hand. He then turned to look at Diana and said, "Look, Di. I fell in love with you by accident, which is probably how it's supposed to happen. I never set out to kill you, I promise, only to possess you with my love. But I'm not going to beg you to love me. With me, you either do or you don't. I can't make you do something you're not comfortable with. If you find me creepy or scary, I'll get lost, before I scare you. Remember what I told you about free will? I don't want that, but again it's about how you feel, Di." Crispin dropped his hands back in his lap, fiddled his fingers and just sat there staring at his feet for what seemed to Diana like an eternity. He found it to be more intense just allowing the silence to hang in the air and envelope them in deep thought.

Finally she broke the silence. "Crispin, you don't have to make me love you 'cause I already do, you big dummy, despite what Sister Lori has told me about you. I'm an adult now and don't feel the need to be a people pleaser. I feel the way I do until I don't anymore, and I consider myself a smart girl, so we'll just play it by ear, okay? If I have any more questions, I presume I can ask you, right? I'm not a total idiot, either; I expect we'll argue, fuss and fight like any other couple. Open, honest communication is essential in any relationship, though. Promise you'll be honest with me?" Diana stared at Crispin with sad doe eyes and poked out her bottom lip, then smiled at him. She crawled over the pillow and pecked him on the cheek.

Crispin nodded and kissed her forehead. He couldn't help but thinking what a drag it was to maintain a relationship, giving up his footloose lifestyle, but at this point he wouldn't have it any other way. He felt fortunate that, being a demon, he didn't really have to engage himself so intimately in the lives of the souls he intended to destroy. Diana was by far an exception, since he no longer wanted to destroy her soul. Winning her trust and love proved to be more complicated than he'd expected, however, the benefits of having someone seriously in his life far outweighed the occasional discomfort of a relationship. *Patience will pay off,* he told himself.

After they conversed a while, Diana snuggled into Crispin's arms, and they chose an action movie to watch on Netflix. Crispin could sense some internal struggle emanating from Diana, but presumed it had to do with their argument earlier and not that she was considering breaking up with him. He was just happy to be there and didn't let it bother him.

Ultimately, they dozed off and abruptly awoke during the credits. They had gotten quite comfy on the couch and soon they were both sound asleep. They giggled and headed to bed to sleep the rest of the evening, cuddled together. Crispin was so happy to have Diana back in his grasp and back in his life, yet he wondered how long he could keep up the charade of never allowing her to see his demon side, he dreaded accidentally exploding into an angry display of emotion. It was clear now that Diana had given him permission to be in her life, which is what he had always hoped for. Now he just needed to work on her other personal stances in life. He was aware of Diana's fervent belief in God, for example. There was no doubt in his mind that he loved her, but his love wouldn't be complete without total possession of her mind, body and soul.

When they awoke, Crispin squeezed Diana gently and nuzzled her neck, preparing to make love to her before she changed her mind. Soon they were consumed in hard, passionate kissing and fumbled with one another's clothing to get naked as soon as possible. Diana was wild with reckless abandon as she scratched and clawed at Crispin's chest, back, and muscular arms, encouraging him to take her any way he wanted. *No doubt, make up sex was always the best,* she thought. Crispin totally rose to the occasion and was all too happy to resign himself to her lust. For hours they made love, played, talked, like they were wild animals. They took a short break to go out and grab some Chinese carry out, they had called in, before they were back in bed again.

They consumed an entire bottle of expensive wine that Crispin had brought over with the roses that night. They were delirious with each other, without a single worry. All disagreements were lost or forgotten. The room was soon full of the strong aroma of fried rice, egg rolls, wine, and sex. Diana just couldn't seem to get enough of Crispin, and he couldn't get enough of her either. Lust was hot and heavy in the air, forbidding Crispin to leave. She finally pulled away to crank open the window but quickly returned.

However, Diana's alarm rang to warn her to get ready for work, so she begrudgingly pulled away from Crispin again to hop into the shower, but he followed her, unwilling to release her so easily. He begged her to stay, but pulling every fiber of her strength together, Diana thought of her mortgage and the cost of staying home. Besides, exotic dancing didn't allow for sick pay. Strippers, by law, were independent contractors and not employees. It was simple. No work, no pay. Unlike Jessie, she wasn't the type to ask her boyfriend to pay her bills. Crispin nodded in agreement and mused over his plans of a higher-paying position in the firm he worked at, now that their manager was no longer going to be in charge. He would be able to ask Diana to quit her job and allow him to take care of her.

Chapter 21

The following morning, Diana leapt up from bed after pushing Crispin's arm off of her and remembering to go to confession—something she hadn't done in a while. But today she felt compelled. Besides, she'd promise her mother that she'd try to go more often.

"Whoa, baby. It's Saturday, where are you going so fast?" Crispin rolled over to look at Diana through groggy eyes. "I've never seen you move so fast before unless you were late to work." He seemed genuinely confused as he watched her.

"Yeah, but I told my mom I would make a better effort to go to confession, so I'm trying to get over to the church before the priest leaves at one o'clock. No big deal, here's your laptop just play with your stocks and bonds til' I return, or something. I'll be right back for lunch. Don't even get up. I gotta run. I'll catch some coffee on the way; love you!" She grabbed a hair scrunchie off of the dresser and threw her hair up in a messy bun then snatched her sweats up off of the floor.

Diana grabbed her purse from the back of the chair and bent over to kiss Crispin good-bye. He quickly grabbed her and kissed her deeply. Then he pulled her down onto the bed, causing her to drop her purse and bag onto the blankets.

"I don't think you're going to have time to go to confession, baby, 'cause I got other plans for us today. There's someone I want you to meet, he's a really good friend of mine." Crispin smiled smugly while nibbling on her ear. Clearly he had no intentions of letting her hook up with her local clergyman, but Diana seemed persistent, and he didn't know why as she pulled away from him, grinning and waving her finger at him.

"No, no, not now, Crispin." She smiled back teasingly but desperately wanted to get away to speak with someone in the spiritual know.

Crispin pouted at first, and then in an unexpected blur of speed, he was standing in front of the door, blocking her way, and wearing a sexy, devious grin on his face. Diana's jaw dropped in sheer awe.

"How the hell did you just do that, Crispin?" Diana began to slowly pick up her things and walk toward him, feeling a bit queasy now because his reaction had been completely unexpected.

"Oh, the little transport thingy? Yeah, one of the many talents of angels—well, demon angels, in your case, baby. Don't tell me you don't find that a little bit sexy."

He swaggered over to her with a big happy grin on his face. Diana sat down in a nearby chair, shaking her head, refusing to embrace him. Then she looked up at him and saw his eyes beginning to change color. But, holding her own, she dared look at him, though he was beginning to creep her out a little.

"I'm not sure exactly what to call that, Crispin, but I think I found it more scary than sexy. Anyway, if you keep this up, I won't be coming back, so just move aside and stop dragging this out please."

Finally, Crispin moved out of the way, gave her a quick peck good-bye, slapped her behind, and said, "Okay, you're right. I'm just messing with you. Hurry up and get back," he teased her and headed toward the coffee maker. "You want me to make you some coffee before you go, dear, save you a few bucks?"

"No thanks, sugar. I just wanna get this over with. I'll grab some at Starbucks over by the church. Love ya. Bye."

Diana hurried out to her truck, jumped in, and took off down Crispin's curvy driveway. He watched her leave from his front room window. She pondered about what had gotten into Crispin this morning. He apparently was not thrilled with the idea of her going to visit the church. However, she did occasionally go to church still—she was still a Christian, after all—but she never expected that Crispin would want to be invited; since he was an atheist. Perhaps she could get him to change his mind.

As she pulled into the parking lot of St. Thomas Cathedral, she straightened her sweatshirt, hoping it concealed the fact that she was braless, then patted up her hair, took a deep breath, and headed through the massive door.

The church was dimly lit inside and smelled of burning candles and leather from the pews that had been recently reupholstered. Diana headed straight for the small confessional booths off to the side, trying to ignore the strong sense of dread building inside of her.

She quietly stepped into the booth, knelt down on the little bench, and waited. Soon she heard the priest enter from the other side of the screen, and she began.

"Bless me, Father, for I have sinned. It's been a year since my last confession. I know being too busy is not a good excuse." She heard a moan of agreement through the screen.

"I'm still an exotic dancer, but I still believe the good Lord has something better awaiting me, so this just tides me over until then. I don't drink a lot while I'm working, and I also don't use drugs; I know better."

She heard another moan and then a chuckle.

"I have begun dating this fellow for the past few months. He's been really great to me, but recently I learned he is half demon. So this lady from my mother's church keeps calling me and warning me to stay away from him, but I don't know how to because I love him, and he says he loves me too."

Now she heard a groan from the priest's side. "He's a liar. That's what demons do, my dear. I'm surprised he was even honest with you about that. Clearly he wants to gain your trust. However, your mother's friend is right. You should get away from him."

His words sent a chill down her arms.

"But maybe I can change his mind, even though he says he's an atheist," she pleaded through the screen.

"No, honey, I'm sorry. It doesn't work like that. Come out to the pew and sit with me so we can talk about this further."

Diana and the young priest exited the booth simultaneously and smiled at one another. She was surprised at how young and handsome he was, but she tried not to be distracted. The priest was equally taken with Diana's great looks, he tried to avoid noticing that she seemed quite busty under her sweatshirt. She still had a bit of bed head and no makeup on; she hadn't been concerned with her looks when she headed out to confession.

As they turned to face each other, they both appeared a bit shy at first, since it was uncanny to make a confession face-to-face. But Diana started in anyhow.

"This guy I'm seeing, Crispin, showed up at my work one night. I'd seen him before, but he'd never let me dance for him. One night though, he wanted only *me* to dance for him, and we were totally engrossed with one another. We exchanged numbers, and then he left. I've been taken with him ever since that night. It's the same for him, because we started dating shortly afterward. He never gives me any grief about my job as long as I don't discuss it with him, and he's always the perfect gentleman whenever we go out. I don't know. I sometimes feel like I can't trust him though, like maybe he's not always telling me the truth. It's weird though. He's not really given me a reason to not trust him." Diana found herself becoming emotional.

The priest held out a small tissue box. "Uh, Diana, that's what you said your name was, right?" The priest shifted on the pew and shook his head slowly. "Demons are masters of human desire and emotion. They cannot be honest because it's a complete contradiction of their nature. They are malevolent spirits and desire only the destruction of our souls. The fact that you have chosen to not only befriend one but, much worse, fall in love with one puts you in grave danger. Quite frankly, I'm surprised he's allowed you to live this long; he's clearly got some devious plan set up for you. I cannot urge you strongly enough to get away from his evil grasp, but it won't be easy or fun. No doubt you'll need some help, of a Godly nature of course. I would be quite honored if you'll allow me to help in this matter. You seem like a good person who's just lost her way a bit. But this guy, Crispin, is potentially a big problem in your life. We should take care of him as soon as possible. I'm quite worried for your soul."

The priest took Diana's hand and bade her not to cry. He felt a spark jump within him, he was definitely aroused by her presence, but since he had been sworn to celibacy, he didn't want to touch her for much longer. She was a worldly woman, after all, and quite lovely to behold.

Diana felt like the priest was sincerely concerned for her welfare, and she welcomed the warmth of his touch. It was different than Crispin's in that the spirit attached to it was warm and loving. Crispin's touch wasn't cold, only different, usually a strongly, sensual touch.

She drew back and asked the priest his name. He told her it was Jonathon, and she told him she would stay in touch with him regarding Crispin. In another uncanny move, she hugged him tightly, thanked him profusely for his help, and ran from the church. When she got back into her truck, she decided to head over to Starbucks in order to confirm her lie to Crispin that she'd actually stopped for coffee to grab herself a latte, besides she didn't want to head back right away. She figured she needed to think on what the priest had said while sipping on her latte.

Oh dear, she thought, *how will I pull away from Crispin without giving myself away? I've got to act as normal as possible toward him because he's so sensitive to my emotions, and now I've got to break up with him. I'm not so sure I can go through with this. Inevitably, I'll have to find a good reason to break up with him. Shit, all this time I wanted to believe he was going to be different. Well, he* is *different, that's for sure, but just not a good different.*

Chapter 22

Diana headed back to Crispin's after getting a bagel and coffee, and she thought about her dilemma all the way to his house. Her phone rang just as she was pulling up the driveway. It was her father inquiring where she was. She explained that she'd been staying with Crispin more now that Jessie had moved out and gave him Crispin's number and address for future reference. He attempted hinting about when he'd get to meet this mystery guy, but Diana brushed him off, only telling him that Crispin was a bit shy and wasn't ready to make his acquaintance yet.

Diana was always happy to hear from her father, who cared deeply for and worried about her. Since she was an only child, she felt very close to her parents and them to her. They stayed in constant contact with one another.

After hanging up with her father, she felt she had enough strength to go into Crispin's house and face him again. When she walked in, he was sitting at his dining table in his lounge pants, reading the paper and slurping down his coffee.

He looked over at her and said, "I wondered when you were going to crawl outta that truck of yours and come inside. I waited for a moment by the door, but you didn't come right in, so I sat back down at the table. You okay?" He got up slowly, so lean and muscular like an Olympic swimmer, and embraced her, trying not to spill her coffee.

Damn him for being so luscious and warm, she thought, but she needed to be wary. *Ugh, this is going to be impossible to break up with him*, she mused to herself.

Chapter 23

"Sure, babe. I'm fine. My dad called while I was pulling in, that's all, just checking up. I told him where I was and gave him your number. Is that okay?" she asked him cautiously.

He just nodded and pulled her close. "I was getting worried about you, honey, because you hurried out of here so fast but came back in so slowly."

Crispin held her at arm's length and smiled warmly at her. Then he picked her up and hurried down the hall to the bedroom, as usual, to unleash his frenzy of lust upon her. But this time Diana resisted him, saying she wasn't feeling well and needed to just lay still for a little while. It was probably something she'd eaten the night before, she told him. Actually, she wanted to see how Crispin would react if he could not have her between the sheets whenever he wanted, since it seemed to be his predictable protocol anymore. As she expected, he brooded. Then he suddenly suggested that he make some tea for whatever was ailing her.

He was disappointed, of course, since lust was the name of the game for him. It was the reason he never stressed her about her work; as long as he and other men could use Diana for their sexual arousal and fantasies, they were just being human and enslaved by their own mortal weaknesses—a perfect playground for demons. Crispin was feeling especially confident now that he had expressed his undying love to Diana, because she seemed to have bought it hook, line, and sinker.

He had to admit to himself that he had impressive acting skills. He almost bought his own act.

As Diana lay in the darkness and stillness of the room, with Crispin checking in on her periodically, she couldn't help but think about the young priest, Jonathon, who she'd met earlier that day at church. She wondered if he had ever been intimate with a woman before. It was quite obvious that he wasn't gay, by the way his eyes were watering over Diana's body and he had clearly become aroused by simply touching her and had welcomed her hearty squeeze as she left. She wondered if he was even capable of being seduced, since he'd probably made some spiritual promise to be celibate. It could prove an interesting challenge later if she decided to pursue it, but for now that was not an option; she simply needed Jonathon's help to get Crispin out of her life somewhat peacefully, if that was possible.

When Crispin entered the room again, he was carrying a tray of BLTs and soup for her lunch.

"Sweetheart, you've been in bed most of the morning. I thought I would bring you some lunch and see if there was anything I could do to make you feel better." He smiled warmly at her, sat at the end of the bed, and rubbed her feet.

"Crispin, you're so sweet. You didn't have to make me lunch, baby. I was just about to get up, shower, and get dressed. I know I've been really quiet today since I got back, but you were right, I just didn't feel too well, so I rushed to the chapel to pray."

"Do you really think God hears you when you pray? I think that is the biggest lie people are told to give them hope. I'm sorry. Not to be crass, but praying is a joke. It just doesn't work, and it ticks me off that people believe that hokey shit."

Crispin was clearly agitated by this subject, so Diana took full liberty to irritate him more.

"Hold on a minute, Crispin. By your own admission, you are a demon. So by definition, wouldn't that make you anti-God? Or are you simply an atheist undercover? I mean, if you are a demon and all things in nature have an opposite, how can you be a demon if there is no God? It's unbelievable. Or maybe you just made that up about being a demon because you thought it might scare me away, huh? You don't know me very well at all, Crispin!"

Diana watched Crispin's eyes go dark but decided to hold her ground and not run. This time she would not be shaken. In an instant, Crispin was standing and glaring down at her while she held her sandwich.

"Are you sure you really want to go there with me, Diana, you little slut? Do you have any idea how dangerous I am? How dare you berate me in my own home. Calling me a liar! You bitch! I am so pissed with you right now, you whore! You dumb little Bible-banger! Get your shit and get out of my house before I kill you!"

To Diana's surprise, Crispin was fully enraged now, and his yelling made her fearful, but without her new friend Jonathon around, she felt helpless, so she moved the tray aside and slowly got up and began to collect her things.

Why was he suddenly calling her all of these horrible names? He'd never spoken to her like this before. Did speaking of God really incite this type of rage? He had known she was a Christian before they got terribly close, but he'd never freaked out about it before. Boy, she must have really touched on a sensitive nerve. Diana thought it best to just gather her things and leave quietly; she was no match for this type of anger and rage.

As she was preparing to leave, suddenly she was lifted off her feet and hurled across the room. She smashed into the mirror over the dresser and fell to the floor. Glass shards from the mirror lay all around her, and she could see that she was bleeding profusely from cuts to her arms and legs. She could see some shards stuck into her thighs. In total fear and astonishment, she looked over at Crispin, who was still standing on the other side of the room by the bed. It seemed he had not moved. She realized quickly that he'd supernaturally thrown her across the room without even touching her.

Diana became immediately aware that she was in grave danger and needed to get to the hospital very soon. Crispin rushed toward her to come to her aid, but she threw her hand up to warn him to back off.

He apologized.

"Call an ambulance, you shit! Look what you've done! Oh my

God, I can't believe you, Crispin! Why were you calling me all of those horrible names? Is that how you really feel about me? Wow! You have really done it now! Hurry, Crispin. Call the damned ambulance, please!" She began to cry as the adrenaline faded and the pain came through. All possible scenarios flashed through her mind. What if her father found out? What about her mother and Sister Lori?

"Wait, I'll just take you. It'll take too long to wait for an ambulance. I'm so sorry. Can you please let me pick you up and carry you to my other car, the Jeep? I'll grab a blanket to wrap you in. Oh no, what was I thinking? I promised never to hurt you. I always try to keep my promises. I'm so sorry, honey. I didn't expect to get so angry with you; I just hate the topic of God and what he's all about, how great he is, and everything. I didn't know I was going to go ballistic like that! I'm so stupid!" Crispin ran round the room frantically gathering towels and blankets and mumbling all sorts of apologies and excuses.

Crispin's eyes began to tear up. He seemed mortified by himself but acted to get Diana some help as quickly as possible, knowing full well it could possibly mean jail for him if she decided to press charges. *Maybe he could talk her out of it on the way to the hospital,* he thought. *Dammit, his is exactly what I was afraid of; showing my evil side.* It wasn't time yet for them to break up. He hadn't begun to really use her to her full potential. But it was imperative that she stay healthy, so whatever his personal price, he needed to get her the help she needed. He'd have to think of something quick before they arrived at the hospital.

Of course, she had been right. He knew God existed, but that was the root of all his problems. All of this flew through his mind in a split second as he was trying to process moving Diana to the Jeep. He tossed a towel onto the bed and gently lifted her to the bed first, and then he grabbed a blanket from the bathroom closet and his car keys. Diana began to moan in pain now and tried to manage her blood loss with the extra towels; she was also starting to feel dizzy, but she allowed Crispin to help her. She simply was unable to move without his assistance.

Once they were in the car, Crispin floored it to the nearby hospital: Sunrise. This was the same hospital out of which Diana's father did his primary surgeries. Crispin wiped his eyes frequently as he drove and then turned toward Diana and spoke in a shaky voice.

"I know I said it before, but you don't know how incredibly sorry I am that I hurt you. I broke my promise, and I'm humiliated. I can only hope that you find it in your heart to forgive me because I love you so much, and I can't believe myself."

"Crispin, just shut up and drive. I can barely think right now much less talk. You're an asshole. That's about as much as I can get out with all this pain and blood everywhere. Don't even try to have a conversation with me after you threw me across the room. Clearly you have anger management problems! I'm so glad I knew about it before I went anywhere with you. Hurry up dammit!"

Crispin sped up more and gripped the steering wheel tightly. He could see that any attempt to assuage her feelings right now would be futile. He'd think of something to say once they got inside the doors of the emergency room. Clearly, spinning a lie on demand was not problematic for him.

As they pulled into the emergency entrance, a rent-a-cop jumped out of his booth, waving his arms, and began yelling at Crispin not to block the ambulance entrance.

"Shut up and go back to your booth!" Crispin growled at him.

The pudgy man quickly nodded and returned to his booth under Crispin's glaring stare. Diana shifted in her seat and motioned to Crispin to hurry and get her inside the hospital. Crispin quickly parked in a handicap spot and rushed around the car to get Diana out of the passenger seat. As soon as he picked her up, she began crying again, and so did he.

"Oh, Diana, baby, I'm so sorry. I know you're a mess, but I promise I'm gonna take care of you. Hang on. The doors are opening now."

Crispin tapped the automatic door opener with his elbow and rushed Diana inside, where a flurry of nurses quickly took over, asking him what had happened. Crispin quickly lied and reported that Diana had been chasing the dog around the apartment, trying to catch him for a bath, and in the rush she had run into the dresser, upon which an unattached mirror was sitting, knocking the mirror over onto her, breaking it, and cutting herself all up. Since he had never laid hands on her, he knew they couldn't accuse him of abuse. That's what *he* figured anyway.

Diana, however, was unaware of the doggie story lie, and while being treated, she explained that her psycho boyfriend had gotten angry and pushed her into the mirror on the dresser. This was also a lie, but it allowed her to avoid the uncomfortable discussion of dating a demon. Besides, it was fairly close to the truth, she figured. This incident provided the perfect fuel for breaking up with Crispin, she thought. Shortly after they arrived, she heard a light knock on the door of the private room she'd been assigned. She felt the medication of the pain relievers dripping through her IV, but in a weak, slurry voice she mumbled, "Come in."

Her father peeked around the curtain, smiling at first and then frowning when he saw her.

"Holy shit, Diana! What the hell happened to you? You look like a train wreck."

He walked slowly toward her and took her hand. She only had the strength to smile sadly at him.

"Don't look at me, Daddy. I'm so ashamed. I don't even know how to begin. You wouldn't believe me anyway. I'm too drugged up to talk right now."

Diana's father just nodded and stroked her hair back. He understood the effects of the medication and could see that Diana was all bandaged up. Diana's father, Dr. Racer, was the senior physician attending that night; therefore, he had to be informed of all cases coming into the ER.

Chapter 24

Diana's father knew instinctively that a man had laid hands on his daughter. He could barely contain his fury as he charged out of the room, bumping into Crispin in the hallway. Dr. Racer swiveled on his feet to meet Crispin's stare. Without missing a beat, he swiftly landed a firm right hook into Crispin's jaw, likely breaking it.

Dr. Racer pummeled Crispin in a mad fury until they were both rolling on the floor together. Finally, nearby officers pulled them apart, and nurses grabbed hold of Dr. Racer. Diana had already described Crispin to her father, so it had only taken a nanosecond for him to recognize him and react. Crispin found himself completely caught off guard. He instinctively went into defense mode. He defended his face and jumped up fast, ready to brawl in the hallway.

"You son of a bitch! Who do you think you are, putting your hands on my baby? You lousy bastard! What, you didn't think I was paying attention? I'd better never see your ass again!" Dr. Racer lunged at Crispin again.

Nurses and other doctors jumped in to pull Dr. Racer off of Crispin and hold him back. Police were standing nearby, ready to arrest Crispin for abuse of his girlfriend since Diana had already disproved his doggy lie. Dr. Racer finally pulled himself together and stormed down the hallway the opposite direction, rubbing his hand and murmuring expletives to himself. Crispin smiled deviously, planning his next move as he was read his Miranda rights and was cuffed by the officers. He couldn't believe he was being placed under arrest for domestic violence. He would bide his time and play the game. He figured that even without using his supernatural powers he could seduce Diana back into his life. He would just simply wait it out. He knew she still loved him.

Diana was completely unaware of the drama that unfolded outside her room, but a few hours later the curtain moved again, and it was Jonathon, the young priest, peeking in on her. He walked slowly over to her bed, gently smiling, and sat down in a chair beside her.

"Well, Diana, it looks like you've had quite the afternoon, huh? I knew Crispin would not have a pleasant reaction to you seeking your faith, but I'm sure glad you're still here with us. The police have already taken Crispin into custody and off to jail, awaiting you to file charges. The nurses explained to the police that your boyfriend had abused you. They explained that he'd thrown you against the mirror at the house. He probably won't have much to say now that your father clocked him in the hallway today." Jonathon couldn't contain his giggle. "I don't usually condone violence, but that was a class act by your dad." He then tried to compose himself and look priestly again.

"What? Did you say my dad decked Crispin outside today? Oh shit! That was definitely not how I planned their first meeting." Diana held her stomach as she tried to laugh, but it still hurt too much. She was still quite achy, though it helped that the nurses had cleaned her up pretty well, before bandaging her.

"Well, I'm pretty certain that was their first and last meeting. You know, I realize that you're all bandaged up now, but I can't help but notice how lovely you still are. Maybe that's inappropriate for me to say. I'm sorry if I offended you." The priest quickly broke his stare and looked down at his shoes. *He hated himself for being so strongly attracted to her.* He scolded himself in his mind about fantasizing about her. *Well, I am only human,* he thought. He could not help but to feel angry towards Crispin whom he'd never met, but felt he knew him anyway.

"No, don't be sorry, Jonathon. You didn't offend me at all. I think you are a very sweet, sincere person, and I'm glad I got to meet you. Unfortunately, every time you see me, I'm a mess. I actually clean up pretty well. You might be surprised sometime, huh?" Diana was feeling less spacy now and more alert as she winked at the young priest. Soon a nurse appeared to take Diana's vitals. She was a robust middle-aged black woman with her hair in braids. She was very kind and quick about her duties. Her name was Gina, and she asked if Diana or the priest needed anything to eat or drink while they waited for the doctor to return. They both politely declined. Then she smiled and left.

"Diana, I brought you a little something, and I hope it will give you a little strength as you pull away from Crispin. It's nothing big, just this little cross on these rosary beads and a little Bible you can carry in your purse." Jonathon laid them on the side of Diana's bed and quickly looked down at his feet. He struggled within not to lock eyes with her, she was even more sexy because she was so insecure about her looks.

"Oh, Jonathon, how sweet!" Diana picked up the small gifts and gave Jonathon a big smile. "But how did you know that I was here?" Diana appeared confused but happy.

"Uh, actually, I make regular rounds at the emergency room throughout the week to check in on patients, so I really didn't know, but I was delightfully surprised to find out you were here. I mean, not happy, but I did want to see you again after we chatted this morning. I didn't expect it to be so soon though."

"Oh really? So this is the same gift you give all of their new patients? A Bible and rosary beads?" Diana winked at Jonathon, who blushed with embarrassment.

"Yeah, you're right. But I do think they will be very helpful. I'm sorry I misspoke." Jonathon looked back down at his shoes again. "You know Diana, God still loves you, though you may have lost your way."

"Don't keep doing that, Jonathon. I want to see your eyes. You have a very handsome face and bright blue eyes, so stop always hiding them when you feel a little nervous. I don't bite, you know," Diana teased him again.

Suddenly, there was a knock on the door. Her father peeked in at her but quickly excused himself when he saw the priest at her bedside. "I'm sorry, I'll just come back, I didn't realize you weren't alone." Dr. Racer quickly exited the room. "No problem, honey. I'll be right outside," he said somewhat tersely. Clearly he was still aggravated by the scene earlier.

Jonathon hurried to his feet and wished Diana good health and a speedy recovery. He then removed a bottle of holy water from his jacket pocket and, after dabbing a bit on his finger, drew a cross on her head and murmured a short prayer under his breath. Afterward, he nodded at her, said good-bye, and told her he'd visit soon.

As he exited the room, Diana's father entered. He had a solemn look on his face, but he couldn't hide the love he felt for her. He approached her slowly and quietly asked if she felt like speaking with him.

She nodded and then apologized. "I'm sorry, Daddy. Crispin's never behaved that way before." She shifted slightly in her bed to remove some of the pressure on her cuts and bruises and then just shook her head in amazement.

"Diana, don't you dare apologize for a prick like him. Now I know why you never introduced him to us. He's clearly nuts! I guess I'm just surprised that you'd even date a fellow like that. I may have broken his jaw out in the hallway a while ago. But nobody's going to be laying hands on my daughter without having to deal with me! Good God!" Dr. Racer ran his fingers through his hair and then stood up to kiss Diana's forehead. "I know it may be too soon to say this to you, Di, but I don't want you seeing him again. Ever again. I know you're grown now, but I'm still your father."

"Trust me, Daddy, when I tell you he's never acted that way before. Believe me!" Diana grabbed hold of her father's hand and began to cry. "I can't believe he got so mad at me when I started talking about God with him. I know religion is a heated debate, but that was just ridiculous; that's all I needed to end this affair for sure!"

Dr. Racer grabbed some tissues from a nearby box and wiped her eyes. "Honey, listen. The staff is going to move you upstairs to a room now. It looks as though you primarily have superficial cuts, however we don't want you getting infected now, so the IV is running antibiotics throughout your system. The doctor upstairs will need to fully examine you. Listen, I love you no matter what, and I will see to it that this jackass stays out of your life!" Her father sat down in a nearby chair but then jumped to his feet again and briskly left the room, speechless.

Diana knew her father was not a man to be toyed with, but then again, neither was Crispin. So she decided not to go into details about Crispin's true nature with him. What a revelation it had been to finally see his true colors, she thought as she considered all of the warnings from Sister Lori and her new friend Jonathon. But they just didn't know Crispin like she did. Secretly Diana felt like Crispin was still salvageable. She still honestly felt he was special and just struggling with his identity. Her thoughts were interrupted by a small crew of staff who'd come in to move her upstairs to a room. In all the rustling about, she asked the nurse to give her some more pain killers so she could rest for a bit. The nurse quickly administered some medication into her IV bag and prepared to take her to the elevators.

She lay quietly on the bed as they rolled her away and took notice of other patients throughout the emergency wing. She caught a quick glimpse of Jonathon sitting by another patient's bedside. *He must stay pretty busy visiting sick or hurt people all week*, she thought. *What would my life be like if I was with someone like him*, she wondered. *Well, I sure as hell wouldn't be an exotic dancer!*

Soon they arrived at the second floor, or Women's World as it was referred to, and she was quickly hurried into a room by the nurse. The room was pink with flowered wallpaper border around the top, and it smelled sanitized, like everything else in the hospital. The curtain was drawn to separate Diana from her roommate. The redheaded nurse, Emma, told Diana she'd bring her some water and that she would begin to feel drowsy soon.

After Diana was finally settled into her room, she dozed off as the medicine kicked in. Diana thought she could will herself to stay awake, but she lost the fight. Nurse Emma tiptoed in and sat a cup of ice water on the table next to Diana. She was very careful not to disturb her rest.

Chapter 25

A couple hours later, two uniformed police officers were standing at the foot of her bed, sharing notes and whispering between themselves. They looked up and saw that she was awake. They greeted her quickly.

"Uh, Miss Racer, are you able to speak with us for a few moments about your boyfriend, Crispin, whom we have in custody currently? We were informed by one of the nurses in the ER that you admitted that he'd thrown you against a mirror at his house in a moment of anger. But we need you to verify this story before we can proceed with this case." The first officer was shorter and older and spoke with authority as his belt buckle struggled to remain in its hole.

"Uh, yeah, Officer. That's right. He was really cool at first. He brought me lunch in bed and everything. Then we started talking religion, and it all went to hell from there. It totally freaked me out because I've never seen him lose his temper like that. I got up to start packing my stuff so I could go back to my own place. That's when he hurled me across the room, and I smashed into the mirror. I was so frightened, but he insisted he could get me to the hospital faster than us waiting for an ambulance. Actually, he was driving pretty fast, and we got here really quickly. But I was afraid of him all the way. I'm so done with him; his behavior was unacceptable. Now what do we do next? Do I press charges?"

"Well, Miss Racer, Crispin tells us he never touched you outside of bringing you lunch in bed and driving you to the hospital," the second younger, taller, more fit officer spoke up.

Diana was too tired to even bother to remember their names.

"Clearly, we have conflicting stories, but in general the law finds itself on the side of the woman. Thought I'd just let you in on that fact. Besides, we thought the dog bath story seemed a bit hokey. We've heard them all by now, as you can imagine." He looked over at his partner and rolled his eyes.

The officers stared at each other for a moment. Then, after scribbling down a few more notes, the older officer finally spoke up.

"Miss Racer, we'll have to call back to headquarters first and make sure your boyfriend didn't already post bail. In general the judge will require a hearing before setting bail but not always. This case may differ, but I'm pretty certain we can find a way to keep him away from you if need be. You are obviously terribly injured and here at the hospital, so your case is up there with severe abuse. The law heavily frowns upon domestic violence. Ever since O.J.'s trial of the century, we've had to really step it up."

"Okay, first of all, we don't even own a dog! What a load of crap he told you! I'm sure he's posted bail already. Crispin's got plenty of money! So if he's out, what does that mean for me? I don't trust him not to come back here and finish me off! Although I must admit, he's usually extremely protective of me and always looks after me; that's why this sudden shift in behavior really frightened me, because he's such a good guy, you know?" Diana was still terribly frightened that Crispin was out and about. She knew he had stepped out of character, but she wasn't entirely certain about leaving him. She wanted to believe he was still a good guy, although she told the officers and her father what they wanted to hear. This didn't change the fact that she was extremely angry with him.

"Excuse me. I'm Dr. Spears, and I'll need to get in here, officers, in order to do a full examination of my patient. I'm sorry to intrude, but clearly this is important as well," a tall, handsome black man in a white doctor's jacket interrupted. He appeared eager to rid the room of the officers and get Diana's evaluation under way.

The officers quickly stepped aside and excused themselves.

"Thank you, Miss Racer. I believe we have all we need at this time. We have your room number and will stay in touch with you, should we need anything else. You will also be assigned a case worker should you ultimately decide to press charges. But right now, we recommend that you get some rest."

With that, the officers hurried out of the room to allow the doctor to do a full workup on Diana. Dr. Spears had warm, comforting hands, and he was very gentle as he removed some of her bandages to check out the cuts and bruises. He continued to mumble under his breath at his shock at her wounds.

"You know," he began, "for the life of me, I don't understand what a woman like you could see in an animal like him, who abuses you. I mean, you seem like a decent person and obviously a pretty girl, but why him? Is it because he proclaims his undying love for you and says he'll never hurt you again? I don't even know this guy, but he's an asshole if he thinks this is okay." Diana frowned and said, "Great, you sound like my dad now."

"Well, sorry, but I'm inclined to agree with him, but let me just continue looking you over." The doctor was not interested in why Diana would choose to defend her boyfriend versus listen to her father. Dr. Spears gently removed a small glass shard still sticking out from Diana's thigh after he removed a bandage. He continued shaking his head again as he patted her foot and half smiled at her. He made a few more notes in his folder before he turned to leave

"Honestly, Doctor, my boyfriend has never laid a hand on me before this. I'm in shock myself. I never saw it coming. I'm not just saying that to defend him either. He showed a side of himself that I've never seen before, but oh, I'm so glad I did before things got any deeper between us. There is no way on God's green earth I'm going back with him again, and I hope he doesn't sneak back in here and find me, either. Yeah, he says he loves me, but this is not a great way to prove it. Besides, I preferred it better when he took me to dinner and the shows." Diana's gaze shifted to the clock on the wall, and she wondered if the doctor believed her fervent statements against Crispin because he didn't appear terribly convinced. She felt that if others only knew Crispin the way she did, maybe they would understand him better, but it was a secret she'd never been comfortable discussing outside a select few people. "I wonder how long I've been here already. It seems like forever." After the doctor completed his exam of her wounds, she thanked him. then she rolled back over and tried to rest.

The doctor checked his folder and then his watch and said, "Well, you've been here for around three hours so far, and I'm going to need to keep you overnight so we can get enough antibiotics into you and also keep you under observation. You'll be free to check out come morning, dear."

Chapter 26

The nurse had come in during the examination to take Diana's vitals for the doctor and reported no fever and excellent blood pressure. However, having to stay overnight panicked Diana. At first she denied that she was too injured to go home to her parents' house so Crispin would initially be unaware of her whereabouts. But the nurse injected more medication into her IV port, and she became drowsy again.

When she woke, her room was dark from the evening and dimly lit by the moonlight. Diana noticed a silhouette of a man sitting in a corner near a chair in the shadows.

"I'm glad you're resting," he said. It was Crispin. "I've been sitting here for some time watching you, worried that I hurt you. Your friend Jessie came by to check on you. I'm not sure how she knew. And your mom came by too. I'm sure your father called her after he attacked me in the ER." He chuckled and then stood slowly to begin to approach her bed.

"You stop right there, Crispin," she said, somewhat groggily but still adamant. "I don't know who let you in here, but I suggest you get going, you jerk." She became more sober and pissed off as she stared at him. She was fearful too, yet Crispin also had a calming effect on her. She wanted to scream but couldn't.

He came closer and took her hands in his; they were warm, as were his eyes. "You didn't really think I was just going to sit there in jail

135

without being able to check in on you, did you? Look, I haven't said much to you up to this point but, I'm still trying to figure out how to get in touch with my human side so that I can love you the way my father loved my mother. I love you so much; I just couldn't bear the thought of you being here and me not able to see you and not explain myself. Not knowing how you were doing was making me crazy. So after the jail officer dozed off, I slipped out to see you; Obviously I'm going along with this charade of being locked up and unable to escape so I'll have to get back before he wakes up, but I wanted to talk to you a bit before you leave here. I'm so, so sorry. I just feel awful."

You're the best thing that ever happened to me Diana. I couldn't see that at first, but now that I do I want to be a better man. If you'll let me, I'll show you I can be better." Crispin reached over the hospital bed railing and carefully held her hand and she didn't refuse feeling somewhat guilty for pressing him into his wild rage.

"Diana, please don't press charges against me. I need to know that you still trust me and love me too, honey. I'll never ever do that again. I promise. I was out of line, and your father had every right to clock me. I'm glad he didn't crack my jaw before they hauled me away. Um, incidentally, I forgot to mention that my boss had a heart attack and died last week, so actually I'm next in line to run the office, and it would really suck for the fellows if the new boss was in jail and unavailable too. Anyway, I just want to hold you right now. I'm not used to sleeping alone anymore, Diana, you've changed all that for me. Let me slide into bed next to you until you fall back to sleep, baby."

Crispin climbed into the bed with Diana and held her closely to his chest. She did not reject him, for she loved him and missed him too and felt somewhat responsible for what had transpired between them. She'd had fair warning that Crispin wasn't thrilled about the topic of religion, yet she pushed him anyway. *He really is a great guy*, she thought. *I shouldn't have pissed him off like that.*

"Crispin, are you really an atheist? Because I'm obviously not, and I don't want to have to walk around on eggshells around you in fear of my life because I love God and I love you too. Maybe it's not right, but it's what I want. I need to know that you're not going to kill me someday, because that would just make this relationship impossible. Of course I've forgive you, you big dummy, but we clearly have a lot to talk about, since I made it clear to everyone how I felt about you and that I would break up with you. Obviously, I won't be introducing you to my folks like we talked about, and it looks like you're gonna have to ante up and pay my bills for a couple of weeks while I recuperate. I'm too tired now." With that, Diana dropped her head onto Crispin's chest and dozed off again

Chapter 28

Once Diana was asleep, Crispin supernaturally reappeared back inside his cell just as the night watchman awoke again. Crispin pretended to be asleep in his cell as the night guard got up to check on him and the other prisoners in separate cells.

The next morning, Jonathon, the young priest, appeared at the jail to introduce himself and to pay a visit to Crispin, who was just waking up but immediately sensed the presence of the priest.

"Hello, Crispin," Jonathon said. "I'm Jonathon a priest from the local parish here. I'm here visiting on behalf of my friend Diana." Jonathon could see how handsome Crispin was and how a woman could easily be charmed by him. He quickly discerned that Crispin's great looks were part of his evil scheme to seduce Diana.

Crispin's eyes darkened. He sat up, alert, and watched the priest sit in a chair on the other side of the bars.

"There is a very strong chance that she will be pressing charges against you for domestic abuse, and I'd like to know if there's anything you'd like to say on your behalf to her, because I'd be happy to relay it to her." The priest pulled his notepad from his pocket and prepared to write.

But Crispin walked up to the bars of his cell and said in a low, controlled voice, "I doubt Diana will be pressing charges. I don't think you know her very well, and if you're a friend, then why haven't I heard of you before? I mean, Diana has always been pretty open about her friends. But maybe you're her dirty little secret, hmm? Furthermore, I don't appreciate you coming in here and threatening me like this, you little Bible-thumper. I don't have anything to say to you. She knows exactly how I feel. Now please excuse yourself from my presence before I excuse you myself."

Jonathon quickly rose to meet Crispin's glare. "You don't frighten me, Satan. I am a child of God. You will not intimidate me!"

Instantly, Jonathon was levitated above the floor and tossed across the room into some chairs. The other inmates watched in horror and began yelling for the guard to come back into the cell area. Jonathon quickly scrambled to get back on his feet.

He picked up the chairs, grabbed his Bible, and ran out of the room, yelling, "I'll be back, Crispin. You don't scare me!"

The guard ran hurriedly into the area, bumping into Jonathon as he entered. The other inmates yelled at the guard that Crispin was creepy and they didn't want to be there anymore. Crispin calmly walked over to his cot and lay back down. The guard looked over at Crispin, confused and in disbelief of what the others were saying. Finally he sat back down in his chair and began reading his magazine again, every so often glancing over the top at Crispin.

Chapter 29

Once Crispin made bail he headed directly home, and he desperately searched his contact book for a few other friends who were also Nephilim in hopes of getting some advice on becoming more human-like. He was confounded with how to love Diana properly so that he would never hurt her again. Any initial plans he had made to use her in devious and malicious ways were no longer important to him. His love for Diana, no longer surprised him, but now he was consumed with how to love her better. He had never seen it coming. He had been so certain he had control of everything. However, Crispin found that love proved a force even stronger than evil.

If only he could convince her of this, they could go back to being the happy couple they were before the drama broke out. Of course now he not only had to convince Diana but her parents and friends as well. Love was definitely something he'd always avoided because of this very thing.

At her mother's house, Diana was lying in bed, bored, and watching HBO, waiting for Jessie to call her back. She was not interested in speaking to her mother about Crispin again. Her mother just didn't understand.

Her mother knocked quietly and then entered the room with a tray containing an egg salad sandwich and a cup of tea. She looked worried but was happy that Diana was safe at home with her parents.

"Here, honey, you should try to eat a little something now. Okay?" Her mother thought it best not to persist.

Back at Diana's parent's house, she was still in her bedroom when Jessie popped by for a visit.

"Diana!" Jessie yelled loudly as she bounced into the room. Then she quickly slapped her hand over her mouth in shock at the sight of Diana's bandages. "Oh my God! Look at you, girlfriend! You're all wrapped up like a mummy!"

Diana giggled lightly at Jessie's comment. She shook her head that it wasn't as bad as it looked. "Don't freak out, Jessie. It's mostly superficial the doctor said. I'm wrapped mainly to prevent the wounds from becoming infected. Besides, I've got some wicked pain killers! Sit on the bed, and I'll give you the story. You are not gonna believe this, Jessie! I've been dying to tell you the details of this drama! Hurry, close my door to make sure nobody comes in."

Jessie ran over to the door, checked the hallway, quietly closed the door and gave the all-clear symbol to Diana. Then she rushed back over and looked at Diana with big inquisitive eyes.

"Diana, what the hell is going on with you? You're acting really weird. Okay, so anyway, what's the big secret? Please don't tell me Crispin's been beating you up this whole time and this is the first I'm hearing about it!" Jesse appeared appalled by the sheer thought of it.

"No no no, don't be ridiculous, Jessie. Don't you think I would've said something by now, at least to you? This is the first time he's ever lost his marbles like this, but we'll get to that in a minute. Let me start at the beginning. Okay, I first met Crispin at the club one night about six months ago, you know this already, but there's more. I'd seen him once before, but I'd never danced for him except that one night! I swear, Jessie, he totally drew me in! You know how excited I was when I got home later, you were there. I mean, I felt like giving him a free dance just so I could stay with him a bit longer, you know?" Jesse nodded her head in anticipation.

"Yeah, but you and I both know you give away free dances all the time. So what? I mean, you're the only one I know who can afford to do that. So what next?"

Diana was thrilled to finally be able to confess to her best friend and spent the next hour and a half giving the yummy details of her and Crispin's relationship. She told Jessie everything except the part about Crispin being a demon. She first waited to see Jessie's reaction to her story.

Right before Diana dropped the last shoe, Jessie spoke up, "Diana, Crispin sounds wonderful, almost too good to be true. So I don't understand. Why this?" Jess began to shake her head at the details.

Diana nodded at the part about him being too good to be true, and then she blurted out rather uncouthly, "He's a fallen angel, Jessie!" Diana clasped her hands over her ears in disbelief of her own sudden honesty.

Suddenly Jessie grabbed her and gently threw her arms around her. Then they looked at each other and both began to cry and giggle simultaneously. Like two school girls, they giggled almost uncontrollably until a knock sounded on Diana's door. It was a heavier knock than her mother's; it must be her father just getting home from the office.

"Just a moment!" the girls yelled in chorus.

"Diana, it's your father. I think we need to speak, honey, as soon as you're done visiting."

"Okay, Daddy. Jessie will be leaving in a few minutes!"

Diana quickly told Jessie that she would call her on her cell later after her folks went to bed. Jessie nodded in agreement and reached over and kissed Diana good-bye. As Jessie ran out of Diana's room, she bumped into Dr. Racer in the hallway. She quickly excused herself and ran out the front door.

It was then that Dr. Racer entered Diana's room, holding a short glass of bourbon. Gerald Racer was a tall, fit man in his mid-fifties. He went running regularly, was lightly toned, and had a deep furrow in his brow. He was very concerned with his looks, probably because of his incredibly vain, wealthy clientele. However, that was not uncommon in the high-stakes world of cosmetic surgery.

He sat down slowly at the foot of Diana's bed and sipped his bourbon before he spoke. "*Ugh*, baby doll. I love you so much. The thought of someone hurting you vexes me greatly. I just don't believe you'd date a jackass like him. Haven't your mother and I taught you better than this? I'm looking at you right now, and it just makes me angrier at him—"

"Daddy, please don't," Diana interrupted. "It's not what you're thinking at all." She leaned forward to touch her father's hand and soothe him. "Crispin is a really great person. I said something snide and unexpected, and he lost his temper. But he doesn't hurt me when he's angry. I swear. This was the first time, and honestly I probably deserved it. That doesn't make you feel better, I know, but I know Crispin pretty well by now. You have to believe me."

Diana knew her words were falling on deaf ears. Her father was not interested in her defending Crispin. "Look Di, there's no excuse for hitting a woman, ever! Don't you dare apologize for him either. Just wait until I get my hands on him again!" She figured the sooner she ended this conversation, the better for both of them. It was clearly a no-win conversation. Besides, Diana knew she had a lot of thinking to do about Crispin, alone.

"Hey, Daddy, would you mind making me some more tea, please? I'd like to take some pain meds now. It's getting late, and I'm a bit tired again."

"Sure, honey. You want your favorite pomegranate flavor, right? With a touch of honey for flavor? Did I remember it right?"

Shortly, her father returned with her tea and Diana nodded and smiled. Gerald stood up, kissed her forehead, and headed out of the room. Diana breathed a sigh of relief but waited to exhale until her father had officially eaten and gone to bed for the evening.

Chapter 28

"Crispin, this is possible to do," said Jacob, another Nephilite. They were speaking at his home while they sipped expensive beers and watched football on Crispin's very large flat-screen TV.

"It's not going to be easy, but you've already made it this far, dude. I mean, maintaining a relationship with a human woman is really tough work, but you've allowed yourself to experience love now. That's something the rest of us flee from big time but not you. I brought this little guide booklet over for you to peruse in your spare time. It's called the *Cambora*, and it's supposed to be a guide on how to love humans and keep your demonic side under control. My father was just like yours, man; he fell in love with my mom, who was human. He told me once that having this little booklet made all the difference in the world. Let's face it: we're afflicted with this drama thanks to our forefathers, but so far I've managed to avoid it. Knock on wood, as they say."

Jacob slid the little booklet across the coffee table to Crispin, who snatched it up immediately. Then Jacob stood, shook Crispin's hand, thanked him for his hospitality and wished him luck.

After Jacob left, Crispin sat alone in his easy chair for a while, flicking through the pages of the *Cambora* guide Jacob had loaned him. It was obvious that several steps had to be taken first to get back into Diana's good graces. The first was repentance of his recent actions, and then when he received forgiveness, Diana would have to consent to giving up her soul for the unforgiveable sin of living and loving a demon. *This is a heavy one,* Crispin thought. *If Diana doesn't agree to choose hell over heaven, we simply cannot not stay together, regardless of what the world thinks.* No other steps could be taken until Diana's love and devotion had been declared. Crispin immediately felt a strong sense of urgency to speak with Diana before her parents and Jessie had a chance to persuade her. Furthermore, after being cast down from heaven himself, he wondered if it was even right to persuade her to give up her soul for him.

He grabbed his cordless phone and called Diana's cell phone, which would ensure his privacy, even at her parents' house. Diana quickly answered on the first ring.

"Hello, Crispin," she answered in a low sultry voice. "Glad to know you're still thinking about me," she said. She smiled. Her tummy had leaped with glee at the sight of his name on her caller ID.

"Of course, baby. I never stop thinking about you. After all, my dick still jumps inside my pants when I think about you. I crave you constantly, like an alcoholic or something. Diana, it's awful having to sleep alone tonight, but I realize I can't come and get you. I can't believe what I did and all of the horrible things I said out of anger! I can only hope and beg for your forgiveness," Crispin pleaded, his voice cracking slightly. He was amazed at his newfound level of human emotion. He was also thrilled to hear Diana's voice and to know she wasn't still angry.

"Crispin, I know that's not like you. I've literally spent hours alone with you, and I've never once been afraid of you, except that time when your eyes turned black in front of sister Lori. Now, getting my parents or friends to believe that is a completely different story. They seem to have this impression that you're going to kill me or something. They also think you've been abusing me this whole time and that I've been covering for you. You'd think they'd know me better by now, but I guess not. I still love you too, Crispin, but we clearly need to discuss some things. I have an idea. Why don't you just supernaturally transport yourself here so we can still sleep together tonight?"

"That's a great idea, but I don't know where your parents live. Why don't you give me the address?" Crispin was greatly relieved that he would be sleeping with Diana that night and that she wasn't still angry with his momentary lapse of reason and behavior.

"Well, my folks live on the edge of town too in a gated community called Ember Oaks. The address is 600 Ivory Coast Lane. So come on over in about an hour after my folks go to bed so we can talk, okay?"

Diana was pleased with her somewhat devious plan to see Crispin unbeknownst to her parents. What would she say? How should she respond? She was a bowl of questions, but she figured everything would just come naturally; it wasn't a stage show, after all.

Chapter 29

Diana rolled over and fell back to sleep but was awaken by her mother knocking on her bedroom door.

"Diana, are you okay, honey?" Cynthia asked, concerned. "You haven't eaten much, dear."

"Thanks, Mom. I'm good. I'm not really all that hungry right now. But if I do get hungry, I feel well enough to go downstairs and get something, so just go on to bed now. I've got good drugs, and I think my scars will heal pretty well. I've got some really expensive scar cream I purchased when I had my boobs done. I'm good. I love you, Mom. Goodnight." She blew her mom a kiss and turned off her lamp.

"Okay, baby, fine. But if you need anything, please holler. We're just down the hall a bit. If you're in more pain, your father will be happy to call in something for you. Okay?" Her mother blew her a kiss back and said goodnight. Then she pulled the door quietly closed.

Meanwhile, Diana just hoped they would go to bed now so Crispin could come over and they could talk. But her father was next. He peeked in after softly knocking and said goodnight, blowing a kiss as well.

After Diana was disturbed by her parents, she rolled back over and waited for Crispin.

"Are you ready to talk now?" a voice mysteriously came from the corner. It was Crispin's voice, but she couldn't see him. "I've been watching all the fussing over you since you gave me the address." His body began to materialize before her eyes.

"Oh my gosh, Crispin! I didn't even know you were here. You were so quiet and invisible too, dummy!" Diana got a tingly rush up her spine, and immediately her nipples perked up with excitement.

She slowly lifted herself from the bed and slightly hobbled toward Crispin, who reached out to catch her before she fell. They embraced warmly, and immediately their tongues met in passion. Crispin picked her up and carried her back to bed, but Diana didn't want to go.

"No, Crispin. I'm so bored of being in bed all day. Just sit me down over on the lounge chair. I can sit up all right."

But Crispin would have none of it. "No, Diana. We need you to get better as soon as possible. I've already done enough damage. Besides, I'm here now, so you won't be bored anymore. I must admit only you could wear bandages and look that hot."

Crispin winked at her and kissed her forehead. He pulled her closely, and she could feel his arousal as he lay next to her, spooning himself around her. *Mmm*, she had to admit that he sure felt good. It was good to be back in his arms again. He nuzzled her neck through her hair.

"Oh, Crispin, it feels like it's been forever since I last saw you. Everything is such a blur. I'm so glad you came. It's so hard to try to explain to everyone that you don't typically beat me up or throw me against mirrors! *Ugh*, I'm so exhausted with all of this! Thanks for coming, baby. I know you didn't mean it. I was so eager to see what would happen if I goaded you … It was stupid. But I can't be afraid of you all of the time if we disagree about something." Diana shifted in Crispin's embrace and turned to meet his eyes.

He squeezed her even tighter. He felt awful. She seemed much smaller, weaker even.

"Diana, baby, the last thing in the world I ever want to do is to hurt you. I was appalled at my own behavior. I've been crying about it all day. Finally, I asked my friend Jacob, another Nephilim, to come over. He was really helpful, but he also thought I was a fool for falling in love with a human, like his father and mine too. But he was still very supportive and loaned me a special book to read called the *Cambora*. He said it would teach me how to love a human without making a complete ass of myself." Crispin seemed happy, but then his smile turned to a frown as he contemplated the rest of the story.

"That's so great! When are you gonna begin reading it?" Diana was happy too. But she was ignorant as well. Nothing was ever as easy as it seemed.

"Well actually, I've already started reading it. It's pretty deep though. After an hour or so, I couldn't read any more. I had to see you. Do you feel well enough to make love with me? If not, that's fine. I'm just so excited to be lying next to you." Crispin tried to evade the discussion about what Diana would have to do to keep them together.

"Crispin, of course I feel well enough to make love to you. Besides, it's even naughtier since my parents are right down the hall. You know, I'm sorry too for getting you all roused up earlier. We wouldn't be here right now if it weren't for me. So I ask for your forgiveness too, baby."

With that, Crispin pulled her close and gently removed her panties. They snuggled in Diana's bed most of the night, with Crispin entering her repeatedly until they were both exhausted. At four in the morning, she didn't want him to leave, but neither of them wanted to get caught by Dr. Racer.

"Crispin, last night was wonderful. I love you. We'll see each other again soon. I promise." Then Diana let him go.

Shortly after came a soft knock on the door. It was her mother asking if she could make Diana breakfast. Diana was still reeling from her fantastic evening with Crispin and the lovemaking magic he had brought with him. But now she'd have to make it through the day without seeing him again. The thought of not having Crispin easily accessible was depressing.

Diana made her way down to the kitchen, where her mother was making breakfast. She sat at the counter.

"So whatcha makin', Mom?" She was glad she felt well enough to be mobile again and was sure it was because of Crispin's lovemaking skills the night before.

Her mother looked over at her and smiled. "I'm just frying up some eggs for you, dear. If I remember correctly, you like them fried over easy for better sopping, right? I feel like I need to get some more food into you. I mean, Diana, even Jesus had to eat. You look so thin, honey, with the obvious exception of your breasts, of course." Mrs. Racer blushed, winked, and turned back to the eggs frying in the pan. "Mom, you don't have to be embarrassed to say 'breasts' in front of me!" Diana couldn't help but giggle at her mom. "I mean at this point I've heard just about every form of the word 'breast.' So trust me when I say don't be embarrassed!"

Mrs. Racer only shook her head and smiled as she slid Diana's breakfast over to her, complete with a side of bacon, a cup of juice, and a slice of banana bread she'd made the previous day.

Chapter 30

After breakfast, Diana headed over the overstuffed sofa in the family room and turned on the TV. After channel surfing for a bit, she landed on Oprah and decided to hang out there for a while. Oprah was interviewing Angelina Jolie and Brad Pitt about how they managed their large family and still kept their sanity.

Diana was surprised her mother hadn't badgered her about Crispin this morning. However, she had noticed that her mother had been going to chapel early in the mornings for prayer. But today she seemed content to just feed Diana and keep her in her presence a bit longer. Diana knew her mother got lonely in their huge home all day. She had friends in a book club she'd joined and a few friends from church and her prayer group. Occasionally, Diana pulled away from her daily life to take her mom shopping at the nearby casino mall. Diana's mother was not thrilled about her current profession but maintained a lot of self-control by not speaking about it very often. Only occasionally did she inquire as to whether Diana was planning to work out of town in the near future, but then she would drop the topic after reminding her daughter that she'd always be praying for her and that Diana should stay in touch and be careful.

Diana stayed with her parents for a week of recovery and had nightly sexual liaisons with Crispin. She was itching to leave and get back to her own place again. Her scars had begun to heal up quite nicely, but there was still evidence that something had happened. She figured she would just lie and tell her customers that she'd been in a car accident but was primarily unharmed outside a few scrapes and bruises. She was up and around her parents' house regularly now and feeling quite capable.

Her mother still insisted on cooking for her; however, her mom's cooking wasn't lean and healthy. Diana was sure she'd gained several pounds while staying at her parents' house. It was only a matter of time before her mom's banana bread, apple pie, and Tollhouse cookies wrecked years of healthy eating and personal training. So one particular morning, Diana got up, took a shower, and washed her hair as usual. Then she asked her mother to drive her to Crispin's house to pick up her vehicle.

"I'm not so sure we should be stopping by Crispin's so soon, honey. I mean, what if he's at home and freaks out on you again?" Her mother seemed very concerned, almost frightened for her. She had no idea that Crispin and Diana had made up and were still seeing each other regularly in the evenings. "Do you still have your car keys with you?" Cynthia seemed wary of Diana's sudden urge to leave.

"It's okay, Mom. Crispin is at work by now, and besides, he's the new boss, so he has to go in. And yes, I have my purse and car keys with me, but all of my other personal products are at my house," she lied, "so I need to get home. That's why I need my car. I've missed a week of work and two training sessions with my trainer, which I will need to pay for now. So anyway, will you be able to give me a lift or what, Mom?"

Diana had grown tired of her mother's worrying and wanted to no longer be under lock and key, but she sensed her mom's good spirit, which was reassuring. So Cynthia grabbed her jacket off the wall and her purse from the kitchen chair, and they headed out to the car, a burgundy Cadillac CTS. It was apparent that she didn't think it was such a great idea, but she held her tongue and decided to choose her battles.

As they headed down the long driveway away from the beautiful mansion Diana had grown up in, Diana couldn't help but feel saddened slightly that she was leaving the refuge of her old home. She reached over to her mother, held her hand, and smiled warmly at her with much gratitude. Cynthia had always been a good mother, and it sometimes made Diana feel ashamed that she had rebelled in this way. She really wasn't able to put her finger on why she'd chosen stripping as an escape from reality and Catholicism, which she felt had been spoon-fed to her since she was a tiny tot. Luckily Crispin had gone into the office that day and would not present a problem for her and her mother. She'd text him later and give him the heads up. As Diana hopped into her vehicle, her mother watched her cautiously.

C'est la vie, she thought. *I moved out to grow up. There's no need in trying to go back now. I can take care of myself. Ultimately, I'll have to consider selling my condo and moving to a less expensive place because I cannot pay that fat mortgage payment alone every month, and I refuse to ask Crispin to help me. I'm not his child. I'm his girlfriend, lover, whatever. Hell, if I wanted to be taken care of, I'd just move back home and let Daddy control my life.*

Diana hopped into her vehicle and pulled out of Crispin's driveway with her mother following closely behind. When Diana and her mother got to her condo to do a quick security check, Cynthia was compelled to come in and see how Diana was living. She gave the place a quick look around and then commented, "Well, it's awfully neat and quiet with your roommate gone, huh? I mean, it looks like you barely even live here. I'd expected to see some dishes in the sink, some cigarettes in the ashtray, or something typical of the single life. But clearly I'm glad to see that your place is neat and clean. You've always taken good care of yourself, baby." Her mother winked at her and gave her a big bear hug, not wanting to let go.

"Thanks, Mom, but the place has also become quite pricey since Jessie moved out. Shortly, I'll have to sell it and move out too." As soon as she spoke the words, she wished she could take them back.

"Oh, honey, don't you worry about paying a heavy mortgage payment. Diana, you shouldn't worry yourself with all of that stuff, besides you'll have to get a really good normal job when you quit dancing to even afford to stay here, so just move back home with us!" Cynthia looked elated. Just the thought of it made her swoon. "It would be so great to have you come back with us!"

Diana, on the other hand, was not feeling nearly as excited. "No doubt, her mom was right, yet she could afford a nice small apartment even with a 'normal' job. Just the thought of living at home again made her skin crawl. She didn't welcome the idea of having to be accountable to her parents for her whereabouts anymore or who she was seeing. Besides, she wouldn't be able to throw a party or anything. God knows sex would totally be out of the question. There would be absolutely no privacy whatsoever. It would be simply be miserable. They couldn't pay her enough to move back home again. True, she could save more money, but the complete lack of privacy wouldn't be worth it.

"Thanks Mom, I'll think about it, I'm just going to run back to my room and get some cash from my safe so that I can grab a few groceries on the way back home. Hang on a moment, I'll be quick."

Finally, they arrived at Crispin's house, and Cynthia was very careful to note all the directions just in case they needed to find him again, she was impressed at how lovely his home was. As they rounded the bend towards his driveway, Diana felt a warm, fuzzy feeling come over her as they pulled into his driveway. She knew he'd gone into work but she desperately wanted to go inside and chill out until he got home. She reveled in thought of Crispin's arms around her once again. She questioned her naivety with him. She wondered if she should heed the warnings she'd been given and just leave Crispin alone. But, what the hell. She felt like living dangerously.

Diana quickly put her things in her Hummer, kissed her mom good-bye, and thanked her profusely for her help and support. Her mother pulled around and waited for Diana to pull out first. It was clear she wasn't leaving until her daughter was safely out of the driveway so that she could follow her home. So Diana rolled her eyes then pulled out in front of her mom and headed down the street. Her phone rang, and she jumped.

"Hello?"

"Hey, honey. I'm so glad that you're free from your parents' house again. I mean, your folks seem really cool and all, but I doubt they want to see me anytime soon." Crispin laughed quietly, then Diana heard a phone ring in the background. "Well, babe, I've got some calls to take, so I'll see you after work?" She could hear the excitement in his voice as they spoke briefly.

"Sure thing, but my mom's gonna to follow me home, so give me a ring there later, okay, bye sugar, love ya'!"

Diana dropped her phone in her lap after speaking with Crispin. Before she called her mom, she had to question herself and her motives. Was Crispin still a danger to her? Could she still trust him? After all, she still had very strong feelings for him, and his friend had loaned him the little booklet on how to better manage himself, so maybe she should give him another chance. But the fact remained that Crispin was still a demon and as far as she knew, that was never going to change. So she picked up her cell phone and dialed her mother, who was following closely behind. "Hey, mom, thanks for helping me get my car, but I know my way home from here, so you don't need to follow me all the way home, okay?" Diana was eager to lose her mom as quickly as possible.

"No Di, I'll just make sure you get home alright," her Mom said with underlying trepidation. Besides, no telling when that creepy guy will show up again!" I'll be sure to hook up with you and Daddy this weekend for brunch and an update, okay?" Diana smiled, and her mother felt it through the phone.

"Okay, sweetheart. That sounds great, but if you have any more trouble with that creepy guy coming around again, you make sure you give Dad and I a heads-up." Cynthia sounded quite adamant as she sped off down the road.

Diana was surprised that her mother had referred to Crispin as creepy. That was the first time she had ever really referred to him. But Diana perfectly understood. She rounded a corner, heading back around Crispin's block. As she pulled up the driveway toward his house, the door slowly opened, revealing Crispin, shirtless, wearing his lounge pants, and looking ever so delectable.

Chapter 31

"Hi, baby!" he yelled to her, rushing to pick her up off her feet and swing her around in celebration of her return.

"Hello, Crispin. It's good to be back in your arms, but I was certain you'd be at work already. How come you're still home, not dressed?" She looked at him, puzzled.

He quickly began tonguing her in the driveway before managing an answer. "Well, it just so happens that the market is closed today. It's Good Friday, and so are we. Which means I have you for three whole days to myself, right? And I'm going to make damn sure that you enjoy every moment of it. I have missed you so much … I can barely stand it any longer. I thought I was going to have to move into the closet in your bedroom if you stayed at your folks' house much longer." Crispin beamed at Diana and squeezed her again. He quickly scooped her up and headed back into the house with her.

Crispin was so overcome with excitement that he couldn't stop kissing her. She tried futilely to resist him but to no avail. He was already naked and removing her panties before she could spit out a sentence.

"Wait, Crispin. Don't you think we should talk first? I mean, shouldn't we know where we stand before we get down and dirty again?"

But Crispin persisted in ravaging her body and shook his head that they didn't need to stop and talk. He didn't want to ruin the mood. It

159

was only moments before he was inside her, so she gave in to his lust and carnal desire.

After collapsing on top of her and nuzzling her neck, he giggled and said, "Now what were you saying again? Something about talking, right? Or were you just thinking out loud?"

He reached over to his night table and took a swig of the beer he'd been drinking when she arrived.

"Crispin, you knew you'd get me all giddy if you took advantage of me. Now I barely remember what we were talking about." Diana giggled at him.

"Well, as I recall, you were the only one talking about talking. But it seemed so boring at the time. All I wanted to do was make love to you without waiting for Mommy and Daddy to go to bed. Let me get up and start us a bubble bath in my big sumptuous tub. Then when can talk in there while I suck on your toes a bit." Crispin quickly hopped up and headed toward the bathroom.

Soon Diana could hear the water flowing and smell the wonderful scent of peaches in the air. She rolled herself in the duvet and took a long whiff of Crispin's smell. Then she closed her eyes and waited. It wasn't long before Crispin was back beside her, snuggled in closely.

"*Mmm*, you smell so good, Crispin. I didn't know when I'd be able to smell you again." Diana rubbed her nose against his shoulder and smiled at him. "I'm really excited to find out what you've been learning about in the little book your friend loaned you. Won't you tell me while we sit in the tub a bit? But don't forget the wine, okay?" She smiled mischievously at him.

He nodded, then quickly hopped up and grabbed a bottle from his wine cooler in the kitchen. He returned with two glasses, naked and wearing a big smile of relief that Diana was home.

They headed into the large bathroom, and he helped her step down into the tub. The water was warm, and the bubbles were high. It felt perfect as she lowered herself into the foamy water next to him.

"Oh, baby, it's so good to have you back. I can't even tell you how much I missed you."

Crispin poured them both glasses of strong wine, and they toasted to her being better and being back. Diana took a sip from her glass and then turned to kiss Crispin passionately, spilling a little wine into the bath water as they heavily made out.

"Crispin, if you don't stop kissing me and licking me, I'll never get to hear about your little booklet. Now tell me how it works, silly. You're acting like a little puppy and I'm your new toy or something. What's the scoop? What do we have to do to make this work? I mean, clearly we have the sex thing down pretty well, but I'm sure there's more to it than that, right? I hope so, but hurry because this wine is going to my head fast."

"Hold your horses, woman. Yes, of course there's more. But I admit that's my favorite part. Don't hate me. Anyway, I've already managed to screw it up a little. But the good news is that you've forgiven me. So that's the first thing. But next is that you have to agree to be totally into me and nobody and nothing else. That's the tricky part and more complicated than I thought."

Diana climbed over Crispin's lap, straddling him, and began to move on top of his arousal. She said, "*Mmm*, that's not so bad, is it? I mean, when I have you all to myself like this, it's easy to be totally into you. I don't even look at other guys, baby. There's just you in my life. I could rock here in your lap all day and night. So I don't see what's so complicated."

Crispin dropped his head back onto the rim of the tub, his eyes closed in ecstasy as he grabbed her behind and moved with her. He wasn't prepared to explain that the nothing else part meant God, as well. He knew it would be just too agonizing, besides being in the moment was all he really wanted right then. Then his head fell onto her bosom. He didn't want to let her go, but he'd have to tell her the rest of the story if he had any chance of keeping her. He fought the urge to lie to her, though it seemed it would be easier. He decided to wait until they had both climaxed. *There was no hurry to ruin the mood*, he figured.

"Diana, the problem is that I can't be anything other than what God created me to be. I'm a fallen angel, which makes me a bad person. I'm considered evil in the eyes of God. And unless you're evil too, we cannot stay together because you need to be willing to convert to my lifestyle in order for me to keep you in it. Put simply, you cannot love God and me simultaneously. Good and evil cannot reside in the same vessel harmoniously. Understand now? So when I say that you have to be totally into me, well, you'd have to denounce God."

Crispin's eyes became worried and slightly tearful as Diana ceased their intimate embrace and slid back down into the tub next to him again. She pouted then sipped more of her wine and began to slowly shake her head at this information.

"Okay, well at least you admit that there is a God now. So that's progress, right? Maybe there's still hope for you, baby, don't be sad okay, we'll figure this out."

Crispin took her chin in his hand and shook his head. He then took another swallow of wine and stood up, grabbing the towel he'd laid on the side of the tub. Diana, still in shock and denial, began to perform fellatio on Crispin while they were still covered in bubbles. Crispin threw his head back and grabbed hold of Diana's head, passionately forcing himself into her mouth before finally falling backward into the tub again, exhausted and sated.

"Oh, Diana, please don't make this more difficult than it already is. I already know what you're gonna choose, okay? It makes me sick to think of losing you, but I have no power over your free will, not even God does. You drive me crazy, and I love you for it. But I choose for you to be happy and not condemn you to hell because of how I feel."

Crispin stood and grabbed the towel again. He reached down to release the drain in the tub and helped Diana up to dry off.

"But wait a minute, Crispin. Are you so sure that you have to stay a demon? Maybe there's a way to turn you into a good angel again? How do you know I'm going to hell anyway? Just because I want to love you and God too? We need to speak to someone knowledgeable about this first before we just give up!" Diana threw her arms around Crispin's neck. Then she took the towel he held out to her and began patting herself dry.

"Wow, Crispin, this wine's got me really tipsy. Can we just go to bed now? I think I've heard enough tonight." She heard her cell phone ring out in the bedroom inside her purse, so she wrapped the towel around her still wet body and ran to catch it. She quickly snatched the phone from her purse. The call was from her parents' house.

"Hey, Daddy," she answered. "Yeah, I know. 'Cause' I'm over at Jessie's, that's why. Um, can I call you guys in the morning? We're getting ready to crash for the night. I love you too. You've been so good to me … I'm feeling much better. Thanks again. Tell Mom I said I said I love her and goodnight too."

Diana looked over at Crispin, who was smiling sheepishly at her and happy she had lied to cover for them, since his jaw still hurt slightly from the right hook he'd taken from her dad earlier. *She looked so incredibly sexy standing in the dim light of the bedroom, still naked and damp,* he thought. Diana had clearly put on a little weight from eating her mother's cooking for a week, but she still looked physically fit. It didn't matter to Crispin one bit, she could do no wrong in his eyes.

What if she chose to leave him because she had been raised to believe in and love God? He wouldn't be able to hate her, after all, but he knew it would completely ruin any chance of a future between them. The human part of him recognized that she had been given free will by the creator, and nobody could change that. Maybe he was just a fool for even falling in love with this lovely creature anyhow, just like Jacob had scolded him. Oh well, the damage was done. All he could do now was let her decide on her own and try to patiently wait it out, just as the booklet instructed.

Crispin gave Diana one of his old T-shirts to sleep in, and then they both snuggled in his warm bed together and held each other closely. Diana could hear Crispin's heart beating, and he sounded every bit human to her. She would ask her friend Jonathon, the priest, for more information, she thought. And being a recent college grad herself, she was no stranger to research. There had to be a way to have her cake and eat it too.

In the middle of the night, Diana got up to get herself a glass of water, and as she walked around the house, guided by the moonlight peeking in through the skylights, she noticed that the Bibles that had been out were no longer visible. She decided to go on a private quest to find them. She felt uneasy snooping around Crispin's house while he was snoring lightly in the bedroom. But she couldn't seem to stop herself from looking around.

She walked down the hallway a bit farther and came to a doorway she hadn't noticed before. She reached out, grabbed the knob, and turned it slowly. The door opened up to a beautiful red room with a small shrine against the wall and several previously burned candles. There was a little table with a Bible on it and a cross hanging on the wall in front of it. This was certainly a surprise and unusual, she thought. What was this room all about? Had this been here before? If it had, she'd never noticed it. But why was it there? And what was it for? Was Crispin actually praying in secret to God, hoping he could be forgiven? Maybe she should pray too.

As she walked closer to the shrine, she noticed the little booklet that Crispin had been given, the *Cambora*. It was turned to the page titled "Demon Forgiveness." Diana smiled and immediately felt her skin crawl for intruding on Crispin's privacy. She thought she should be getting back to bed before Crispin awoke. She figured this was a discussion for later, not one to have at three o'clock in the morning.

She quietly navigated the house and slipped back between the blankets next to Crispin. He gently grinned in his sleep at her return and pulled her close. He was back to snoring in moments. Diana lay there for a while, listening to him breathe and considering the ramifications of what he'd said in the bathtub. Good and evil could not reside in the same vessel simultaneously. This was clearly problematic for their relationship. But was it even possible for her to break up with Crispin? It wasn't like she could just go and hide somewhere and he wouldn't be able to find her. After all, he knew where she worked, where she worked out at, and where she lived. And now he also knew where her parents lived. But he didn't know where Jessie lived. Maybe her place was a possibility.

Oh, I'm being stupid, she thought. *Of course he can find me wherever I go. I can't hide from him, really. But do I really want to hide from him? How do you make yourself not love someone anymore?* If someone was naturally forgiving, which she was, it wouldn't be easy unless that person was poorly treated on an ongoing basis. This was something

Crispin was not guilty of, with the exception of the recent incident. She reached over to her leftover glass of wine, took a big swallow, and tried to get back to sleep.

By this time, Crispin's arousal poked her behind. He was ready to make love again, though his eyes were still closed. Diana hadn't put panties on after their bath, so she happily obliged him for half an hour, and they both dozed off together again. She felt hopelessly addicted to him. *Why fight it*, she thought as she slipped into dreamland.

Buzz, buzz—her phone vibrated early. Way too early for a Saturday morning.

"Yeah, hello?" she mumbled into the phone.

"Hey, Di! You wanna come over for the weekend? Mom and I were going to do some grilling for Good Friday Weekend. I wanna see you anyway. We should talk. I miss you, and I'm worried about you. Are you feeling better? Your mom told me you went back home."

Wow, it was way too early to be having this conversation, she thought.

"Hey, Jessie. Yeah, I feel really great, actually. I was getting bored and cooped up at my folks' house. You know how it is." Diana glanced up and saw Crispin entering the bedroom with breakfast in hand. "My parents are really great, but it's weird having them around all the time. I've gotten used to my independence. I'd love to swing by and see you for a little while. We've got a lot of catching up to do, but I did promise my folks I'd meet up with them for breakfast this weekend, probably on Sunday after service, but I don't want to spend the afternoon with them bashing Crispin though." She sat up and smiled at Crispin, who was placing an omelet, strawberries, and coffee before her on a little breakfast table. *He's so wonderful. I'd be a fool to break up with him*, she thought.

"So, Jessie, I gotta run. What time are you guys going to be grilling on Friday? I'll pop in for a bit. You've always been so supportive, especially since you got rid of that pig, Chad, but you're probably thinking that I've got some nerve, huh? Okay, sounds good. I'll see you around two then, and thanks for the invite."

Diana pressed *End* on her phone and looked back down at the delicious breakfast Crispin had prepared for her. He was all smiles as he watched her eat. Then his expression became sad.

"Crispin, what's wrong? This is delicious. I love it! Don't look sad. So what if you scrambled my eggs instead of fried them? It's healthier anyway. What a fabulous gesture from you." Diana took a big bite of a strawberry and offered the rest to Crispin.

"Shortly after we made love last night …" he began, "I had a horrible nightmare that you decided to leave me and nothing I said mattered anymore."

"I felt so devastated by your decision, but I respected it all the same, and I walked away crying."

Crispin leaned over Diana's plate and kissed her gently on the lips. She could see that his sadness was genuine. She moved her tray to the side and climbed over to sit in his lap and hold him.

"Look, I haven't decided anything yet. So don't go writing me off in your dreams, buddy. I still think there's a better solution to all of this, and maybe your friend Jacob doesn't even know about it. After all, your own mother was human. She clearly made the decision to stay with your father and conceive you, right? We need to do some more research and at least try to fight for our love."

Diana began stroking Crispin's hair and his face, looking deeply into his eyes. Then she kissed him lightly on his ear and repeated to him that he shouldn't worry so much, because everything would be fine. She reminded him that they had been seeing each other for several months now Crispin nodded in agreement, though he wasn't so certain. He squeezed Diana hard and began to cry in a muffled groan.

"No, no, baby." She used the end of her T-shirt to wipe his tears.

Diana was impressed that he let her see him cry. But it also made her feel a bit uncomfortable, since this was the same man who had rescued her from the club that awful night. She knew she needed to see a demonologist at the university as soon as possible. It was crucial that she get answers soon. She wished she hadn't fallen so hard for Crispin because then this would all be unnecessary. But it was certainly too late to turn back now.

She handed Crispin her tray and asked him to make her some tea so she could take some painkillers she had in her purse. Then she told him to come back to bed with her. The most important thing, she explained to him, was to live in the present. Regardless of her decision, they still owned the night together.

Diana's phone rang in her purse. As she got up to get it, Crispin pulled on her, "Please, don't go, Diana ... I love you."

Diana motioned to him with her thumb and pinky finger that she was only getting her phone.

"Hello?" she asked rather tersely, only to gulp hard when she heard Jonathon's voice.

"Hey, Diana, did I catch you at a bad time?" He answered timidly. He felt awful having called to check in on her. He had wanted to call her for an entirely different reason, like dinner.

"Oh, hi!" Diana answered happy, though still caught off guard. "Um, yeah, I was just in the middle of something ... I'll be happy to help you with that, but not right now. Can I give you a ring tomorrow morning?" She hoped he would say yes, though he had no idea what she was talking about. Finally he put it together that Diana was in the company of someone and couldn't speak freely.

He agreed easily.

"Okay, great. I will then." She tapped the *End* button, dropped her phone back into her purse, and turned toward Crispin again, who seemed confused. "That was just an old friend of mine from school. She needs some information about something, that's all. It's not urgent though," she lied smoothly through her full pouty lips and proceeded to sit back on his lap, but he motioned her to wait a moment. He stood and decided to get some wine for them, because now he was horny again and tired of talking. It was just too exhausting and sad trying to figure it all out. But, these necessary discussions never seem to hamper his sex drive as it would most human men.

He grabbed a bottle from his mini wine cooler and a couple of glasses from the overhanging glass rack and headed back toward the bedroom, where Diana was still waiting. "Wow, Crispin, a bit early for alcohol, don't you think?" Diana was perplexed by his actions. "Yep, it is, baby, but I'm feeling a bit stressed right now. I know you just finished breakfast, but would you care to join me?" He smiled flirtatiously to her. "No thanks, I'll just have a short glass of orange juice if you don't mind." No sooner had the words left her lips before Crispin was in the kitchen pouring her juice. *He's clearly going over the top with his guilt,* she thought.

When he returned, he said, "baby, I don't want to talk any more. This is all too depressing for me. Let's just pop a movie in, have our drinks, and make love again, okay?" Diana laughed softly at the idea that Crispin always preferred sex over talking, but then again that wasn't different than any other guys she'd dated.

Diana nodded in agreement, and Crispin proceeded to pour himself more wine.

"What shall we watch today, love?"

"We should watch something funny, Crispin. What funny movies do you have in your extensive collection, over there?" Diana curled up on top of the blankets and gulped down a mouthful of juice. "Do you have *The Wedding Crashers*? I think that one is pretty funny!"

Suddenly, a loud noise crashed outside. They rushed to the bedroom window and peered through the blinds. There had been a car accident in front of Crispin's house. Shocked, they threw on some clothing and ran outside to see what the fuss was about. Apparently, Crispin's friend Jacob had decided to drop in for an impromptu visit and backed into another car from Crispin's driveway when he saw that Diana's truck was there. A frantic Asian lady came out of the next door neighbor's house running n cursing down the driveway. As she swore she waved her small fist in the air at him. She stopped cursing when she saw how handsome Jacob was, however she was too angry about her smashed car to be smitten by his good looks.

"Hey, Jacob. What are you doing over here? I wasn't expecting you today," Crispin asked as he walked over to Jacob, in just his sweatpants and no shirt. The Asian lady couldn't believe her luck that she was now in the presence of two very good-looking men. Diana hovered closely behind Crispin, looking sad about the lady's little blue car.

" It's not like it's a busy street or anything. *Ugh*, just call the police, and let's get this done already."

Jacob grabbed his phone from his pocket and, eyeballing Diana, proceeded to call the police to the scene to write up an accident report for them. Since he drove a Ford Excursion and the woman had a Kia, she had obviously gotten the short end of the stick, even though her car had been parked on the street while she visited her friends. Her front end was pretty well scrunched up, but her car was drivable, and his vehicle barely had a dent. After they waited outside for about forty minutes, the police finally arrived and took the report. The woman, Mrs. Jones, had yet to settle down, regardless of how many times Jacob apologized to her.

"Wow, you sure are a little hottie," he'd said to Diana earlier.

"Thanks, Jacob. Nice to meet you too," Diana had answered rather coolly; amazed that Crispin would allow his friend to speak to her in that manner.

"Well, I can certainly see why Crispin is so twisted up over you now." He had smiled and then winked at Crispin. Crispin had pulled Diana behind him in a possessive way and thanked Jacob. "Okay Jacob, that's enough, funny guy just finish your report and come inside for a bit. He took Diana's hand and they turned and headed back up the lawn to his home. They decided to resume their movie they'd paused before running outside; hoping that Jacob wouldn't stay long since they had plans to continue blowing off the rest of the day in one another's company. Their recent absence from each other had truly made their hearts grow fonder, as the cliché goes.

After the police took their statements and cited the accident. Jacob went up to the house, peeked in the door and stated that he didn't want to interrupt their day anymore and said he'd come by another time. He apologized for intruding.

"I really should've called first, man. I didn't realize you weren't alone. It's not too terribly important. I'll hook up with you later on. You guys go on and finish enjoying your day. I'm really sorry about the intrusion again."

Jacob jogged down the driveway back to his vehicle turned around and took off down the street. He smiled all the way home, thinking about his buddy and his hot girlfriend he was so into. How would he explain to Crispin that he'd have to fully convert to human losing all of his supernatural powers, or that Diana, would ultimately need to sell her soul to be with him? How depressing, he thought. She was definitely very sexy and she seemed cool too. He knew better than to go in that direction with a human. His father had warned him, and so had Crispin's father. Apparently the warnings had fallen on deaf ears when it came to Crispin.

Crispin and Diana headed back into the house, holding hands and talking about what a fluke of an day it had already been. As they entered the house, Crispin took Diana in his arms again and kissed her passionately. His fear of losing her only made him want her more, and he could contain his carnal desire no longer. After quickly and fiercely disrobing each other in the living room, they eagerly made passionate love, rolling around on Crispin's white Flokati rug, while the movie played, mostly unwatched. They were both overtaken by extreme orgasms before they collapsed.

It was late, pushing midnight, by the time they managed to crawl to the bedroom, where they could fall asleep to a late night show in the comfort of the bed. Nothing could tear them apart. They felt invincible.

Around midnight, Crispin's phone buzzed. He could see it was Jacob calling, so he slid from between the sheets quietly so as to not wake Diana and went to the bathroom to speak to him.

"Hey, man," Jacob whispered as though he was supposed to be quiet on his end too. "I'm really sorry I busted up your evening with uh, what's her name? She's really hot, man. But anyway, I figured you'd be alone, and I wanted to tell you something."

"Yeah, Jacob," Crispin whispered back. "Nice job, man. By the way, her name is Diana." What did you need to tell me that you couldn't just call me anyway?" Crispin retorted abruptly. He listened carefully and with total interest at what Crispin was telling him. Ultimately it was too disturbing and he asked Jacob to not tell him any more because he wanted to go back to sleep.

When he returned again, he decided to awake Diana, so he gently nudged her until she turned her head toward him.

"Crispin, baby, I don't want to fuck again. I know it's your favorite hobby, but I just want to sleep, now, okay?" Her voice was soft and raspy.

"No, honey, I don't want to fuck either. I just want to tell you something important. So can you turn over for a minute?"

Diana rolled over to face him. "What's up, sugar? Why the urgency at midnight if not for sex?", as she glanced at the clock on the nightstand.

"Well, I just got off the phone with Jacob, my friend you met earlier this evening, and he explained to me that in order for us to work, I'd also have to relinquish my supernatural powers and become human too versus just you renouncing God, so I guess that was supposed to be a consolation." He looked at Diana and frowned sarcastically.

"Okay, baby. Wow. I don't know what to say," she replied, squinting her groggy eyes at him, but showing no real interest at the moment. "I suppose you have more to consider than you thought, huh?"

Diana did not give this new discovery much thought, so she gave him a quick peck on his cheek and rolled back over. Living without supernatural powers didn't really seem too big a deal to her; actually, it seemed rather normal. Crispin snuggled her again and smiled as he drifted off again. Now he'd have to decide if she meant more to him than his supernatural powers and being "a fallen angel", which was all he'd ever known. How far was he really willing to go with this unique situation in which he'd found himself?

Meanwhile, Diana's father was driving by Crispin's house and spotted Diana's car in the driveway, but instead of exiting his car, he decided to just make a mental note and keep driving. His ex-wife, Cynthia, had given him explicit directions as to where Crispin lived, and he was not beneath playing private investigator on his way home from the hospital.

Great, he thought, *she went running right back to that sleazeball again!* So Dr. Racer headed back home and figured he would bring it up sometime later, since they were probably already asleep by now. He couldn't help but wonder what he had done so wrong in Diana's life that she would need to be with someone like Crispin. Could he really have been that poor of a father, or did her sleazy job have something to do with it? But Dr. Racer had attended a bachelor party for one of the hospital residents at that same club earlier that year, and it certainly hadn't come off as sleazy ... It was a very classy club to say the least with a four star menu to boot.

Chapter 32

When morning finally came, Diana rolled over to see Crispin still sleeping calmly. She smiled and then whispered to him, "I'll do it for us, baby. I don't want us to ever be apart again. Say you'll do it too." Then she stroked his hair gently as his eyes slowly opened to see her.

He felt awash in disbelief yet relieved as well. He pulled her firmly against him and gently kissed her lips. Then he wiped the wake-up sand from his eyes. He wasn't certain if she knew what she was saying or not, but he figured they could straighten it out later over coffee. He knew at this point that he didn't want to be without her either, but he also didn't want her to sacrifice her soul to be with him or for him to be just a regular guy; however, he'd always heard that you couldn't have your cake and eat it too. *Maybe it is true*, he thought. *Maybe love really does conquer all.* This new human emotion was exhilarating to him and yet quite complicated … He understood all of his father's warnings now.

The sunlight beamed brightly through the blinds onto their naked bodies as they yawned and stretched. But one glance at Diana's naked breasts was all he needed to be ready for morning sexercise.

"Come here, you. Look at what you've done to me already. I'm so hard I could cut diamonds. So I believe you have your work cut out for you before coffee." Crispin smiled broadly and slowly stroked his thick cock.

"Crispin, you are such a bad, bad boy, and I love it. It just so happens that I can perform a pretty decent blowjob before coffee. Come over here and let me show you." Diana teased him, but Crispin didn't need teasing; he needed pleasing.

It didn't take long before he was happily screwing Diana in the streams of the bright Vegas sunlight shining through the huge bay window of the bedroom. As they dragged themselves from the bedroom toward the kitchen and the coffeemaker, which had been preset the night before, they continued smiling at one another and giggling about their mischievous morning. They remained naked, freely walking around Crispin's house and agreeing to bathe together later in the morning.

They casually plopped themselves on the sofa. Diana wrapped herself in the throw blanket to block the chill she was beginning to get and looked up at Crispin over her coffee cup. "So what did you decide, lover boy? Are we gonna do this or what? I know that I'm ready ... Just being away from you that week while I was healing made me totally certain that I needed you in my life, and I don't care that you won't have superpowers. So what? I'm fine that you're going to be a normal guy. Besides, you're still drop-dead gorgeous! So when do we begin? Don't worry about my folks either. They'll come around when they see how happy you make me!"

Diana was getting very excited and talkative about the new life she'd have with Crispin. However, Crispin hadn't really made a decision yet.

"Um, Diana, before you get all wound up, I think we should talk a bit first, okay? I'm totally in love with you. I have no doubts about it. But at first I was concerned that you would lose any possibility of going to heaven by being with a fallen angel. Now I'm concerned that those very superpowers I've used to protect you and avenge you in the past may be taken away, and quite frankly it scares me to death. I've only ever known this lifestyle, and the possibility of change terrifies me. But I wouldn't expect you to understand that, I guess." Crispin frowned and looked down at his coffee again.

"Crispin, OMG!" Diana leapt off the sofa, headed toward the bedroom, and began getting dressed and tossing her clothes in her favorite carry-all bag. "I cannot believe this shit! So I'm willing to give it all up for you after six months of all sorts of bullshit, lying about you to friends and family and everything, but you're fucking worried about not being Superman anymore? I know just what you need, Crispin. You need some more time away from me so you can see what it feels like to miss someone you love! Do you even know how much work I've missed just so we could hang out together! Shit, I should have trusted my instincts and not gotten involved with you at all. I knew I would get hurt! Shit! And fuck you, Crispin! Leave me alone until you get yourself figured out, and don't go popping up at my house secretly either or I'll invite Sister Lori to come and stay with me. I gotta get outta here. Go count your money or whatever it is you do!" Diana stormed out of his house and to her car, fuming and crying simultaneously.

Crispin sat there alone feeling like shit. He simply wasn't as certain as Diana was, and she didn't seem understand or want to understand his position. He reached over to the coffee table, grabbed his cell phone, and called Jacob. He invited him out to the sports bar for a beer later on. Jacob agreed, knowing full well what the subject of the evening would be. But that was what friends were for.

Over the loud blasting music of her Hummer, Diana noticed her cell phone ringing in her purse. She reached over, wiped her sniffles, took a big breath, then took the call.

"Hello? Oh hi, Jonathon. No, no, I think its allergies," she said when he inquired about her voice. "No biggie. I'll still be working tonight. Thanks for checking on me though. That's really sweet of you. I'm heading home right now to get showered and ready for my nail appointment and work later, but I'm going to need a nap 'cuz I'm feeling a bit stressed right now. Too bad you can't come and visit me tonight… It'd be good to see you again outside the confession booth." Diana chuckled into the phone.

Chapter 33

"Who says I can't visit you? I can go anywhere my clients go. Not that I consider you an ill patient or anything. I know I'm a man of the cloth, but I'd really like to see you again too, Diana. When does your shift begin? I'll come a bit early so I can have few drinks before we get together, okay?" Jonathon couldn't help sounding eager over the phone, like a virgin.

"Well, unfortunately I work the nine-to-five shift, so that's about when I'll hit the floor. If you want to come in about eight, it'll be crowded, but you can have couple of drinks before I dance for you. I'm sure that having denied yourself for so long, you probably need a few drinks to relax, huh? But I suggest you wear jeans and try to blend in a bit 'cuz that little white collar thingy ain't gonna work at a titty bar."

"You'd be surprised, Diana, at my lifestyle outside the church. I'm still every bit a man. Trust me, I don't wear my uniform when I head out to the grocery store." Jonathon sensed the sarcasm in her voice, which made him even hornier. He'd show her, he thought.

After Diana hung up, she smiled to herself that the priest would come to the titty bar. Boy did she have a confession for him. But it was her turf, so perhaps he should make a confession. And he would. This might be fun, she thought. Then she cranked her music again and went back to thinking about Crispin's selfishness.

As she pulled into her gated community, she spotted Sister Lori leaving. The nun didn't notice Diana turning in. Diana was so happy she had dodged that bullet because Sister Lori was one person she didn't want to deal with now. She rushed into her condo and quickly started some fresh coffee but felt sad that she would have to sell the place eventually. She could only work so many double shifts to cover everything. Besides, it didn't look as though Crispin was going to come through for her, but she could stay at his house while showing hers on the market.

Diana ran a hot bath for herself and then enjoyed a thorough masturbation session while bathing. After her bath, she began swigging her coffee, which had completed percolating. And then she took a nice long, hard look at herself in the bathroom mirror … She felt confident enough to go back onstage, since her scars had healed well. Besides, there was always cover-up for the ones that hadn't healed as well. She held up her breasts and stared at them momentarily; they were still big and sexy, so that hadn't changed. She was definitely still hot, scratches and all. Maybe she didn't need Crispin after all. But that hadn't been the plan. Granted, she would never expect Crispin to maintain her luxurious lifestyle, but he could try for a little while … That's why a girl always stayed in touch with her sugar daddies, after all.

She looked forward to getting back to work and taking her mind off Crispin for a while, but once she arrived, she had to field a zillion questions about her made-up car accident. She put on one of her favorite clingy see-through gowns, and before long she was totally engaged in her dance, closing her eyes periodically as she lay onstage, massaging her body and thinking of Crispin. All the guys ogled her and tossed tips on the stage at her.

Suddenly Jonathon pushed through the crowd of guys and yelled her name. "Diana!" He didn't know that dancers didn't use their real names at work, only stage names.

"That's Candy, you dumbass!" Another customer barked at him.

Jonathon shrank back in delighted ecstasy. Candy had still heard Jonathon over the other drunken fellows, and when her set was complete, he met her at the stairs and begged her to go upstairs and dance for him.

"Hey, Jonathon. I'll go freshen up first, and then I'll take you upstairs, okay?"

"No, Candy. Please, do it now. I can't wait any longer. I'm so wasted. I need to walk back to the church soon and sober up."

Candy could see he was pretty buzzed, so she grudgingly took him up on his offer. He took her hand and headed directly toward the VIP spiral staircase. Candy chuckled at the priest's excitement but promised to give him a good show all the same. She led him over to a corner booth, which was more private, and sat on his lap. She explained that she would not do a typical 'air dance' for him, she believed in full contact dancing, much to the chagrin of management and the other dancers. Jonathon begged her not to be nice to him because he was a priest. Besides, he was already erect and ready. But she explained as she stood up that this was only a dance and not sex, though her dance style was extremely sexual by design.

She headed over to the jukebox to select a few songs to dance to. The other dancers didn't mind because they enjoyed the music Candy selected. Jonathon began stroking his erection through his jeans to be sure to impress Candy when she returned. Once the music began, Candy went into game-face mode and rubbed her breasts in order to make her nipples stand at attention. She began to slowly undress for him, somewhat shy that he was a priest, yet excited as well to make him sin. Jonathon watched eagerly but controlled his hands so as to not make the bouncers yell at him.

"God, Diana," he whispered in her ear as she began to grind on his cock. "Ever since you came to confession, I haven't been able to stop thinking about fucking you. While we were sitting there on the pew together, I just wanted to reach out and grab your titties and tongue your mouth. And then I thought about pulling you back into the booth so you could blow me. God, I'm ashamed of myself, I'm sorry. Please don't think less of me. I'm still a man, and I can't bear the thought of Crispin fucking you and not me! Please, just grind me some more until I come on myself. I just need some release. It won't take me long, because I'm already close. You feel so good, Diana. Please let me fuck you just once. I can still help you with that creep if you want, and I won't ask you for anything else, I swear. I'm so frustrated and embarrassed. But I just can't control myself any longer!" Then Jonathon erupted in his jeans. Candy moved aside and grinned mischievously at him. He smiled a huge smile back at her and whispered thank you to her as he slowly stood up. She draped her dress across her and gave him a one-armed hug with her free hand. *That will teach him to be such a good boy all the time*, she thought.

Candy hopped up to excuse herself to the dressing room. She was kind and pretended not to care, since this wasn't the first time, and it wouldn't be the last. She kissed and hugged Jonathon good-bye, and he smiled at her, mouthed *thank you*, again and slithered out of the club, happy and embarrassed.

Well now, that was interesting, she thought. *I seriously doubt that Jonathon believes I'm going to sleep with him just to keep Crispin away. I don't want to keep him away, but he doesn't know that yet. Jonathan sure was doing a lot of dirty talk tonight; he must've been really tanked. Good thing I hear that shit so much it doesn't bother me anymore.* Candy grabbed her purse, which she always kept close by, already stuffed with cash, and headed downstairs to the dressing room to freshen up and change. She checked her voicemail to see if Crispin had called and checked her text messages too. There was still nothing.

Meanwhile, Jacob was still playing wet nurse to Crispin. "I understand what you're saying, Crispin, but come on, man. You can't expect her to do all of the sacrificing here. It wouldn't be fair. This is an all-or-nothing gig for both of you, dude. I mean, you and I didn't have a choice in this, but she does, and she chose you! Now you want to penalize her for loving you? That's fucked up, dude. You need to check yourself. Stop calling me and telling me how much you love her. Just tell her and show her, unless you really don't and you were just horny."

Jacob and Crispin sat on the barstools in silence for a while, sipping on their beers and watching the rest of the football game on the monitors above the bar. After a beat, Jacob stood, finished off his beer, and gave a hearty thanks, a handshake, and a good luck to Crispin.

"Look, man, I gotta go. Another soul to steal, you know."

Crispin walked Jacob out to the front door and thanked him for coming by and bearing with him.

Back at the club, Candy was enjoying the profits of the evening. Only two customers had mentioned her scars and offered their sympathies about her recent car accident. When she went back downstairs to the dressing room to count her earnings, she went into a private stall so as not to intimidate the other dancers. She had not lost her magic. Eight hundred fifty dollars later, she was all smiles and considered not selling her condo if she could keep her winning streak going. Of course many of her regulars were extremely generous, since she'd been absent. However since her mortgage was only fifteen hundred bucks a month. *She would not allow some man to have control over life, even if it was Crispin, her customers' loyalty would push her through the slow patches,* she figured. Her father had taught her a long time ago not to let a man disempower her. This was advice she took quite seriously.

She hustled back upstairs quickly after fixing her hair and costume, because she was well on her way to making her thousand-dollar quota for the evening. Her shift would end in a few hours, so she went to hustling her dances with fervent pleasure. On her second loop through the crowded club, she bumped into Crispin. He spoke quietly to her, pulling her close and whispering in her ear, "Baby, I love you. I'm being stupid. I know that now. Of course I'll do it too, if it means keeping you in my life."

Candy's tummy rolled and jumped with joy. But she stood her ground firmly. "Look, Crispin, that's all well and good, but I don't know if I can trust you now... You really hurt my feelings. Besides, right now I'm a hundred fifty bucks short of my goal and can't really talk about this now, okay?" Candy tried to pull away but was stopped by Crispin's firm grip.

"Let's go upstairs to the VIP room so I can help you meet your goal, baby. Besides, it's been a while since you danced for me."

Candy swiftly took Crispin's hand, she curtly reminded him that it was only business and escorted him upstairs, stopping ever so briefly to tap a song into the fancy jukebox.

"Now, I should remind you again that the bouncers do enforce the no-touch policy up here, which may be difficult for you at this point in our relationship, but please try, okay?" she chided him seductively.

"Yeah, yeah, I know the rules, baby, so just shut up and dance for me, please."

Candy happily agreed and danced for Crispin the way she first had. Then he asked for another and another. He tipped her fifty dollars for each dance, and finally she made her quota for the night before tipping out her deejay and the house. They both admitted that it was difficult to dance so closely without being intimate and it really sucked but Crispin was more interested in getting Candy out of the club to converse

"So can you leave now, since you made your quota? I'd like to take you somewhere to have a hot cocoa, tea or whatever you drink after work. We could sit and talk for a little bit if you want? Obviously, I want you to come back home to my place, baby. I've been sick since you walked out this morning. I wanted to give you your space, but another week just seemed a bit too much. Please come back, honey. I've had enough time to think it all through. Jacob's father will perform the ritual for me to change over. I honestly know what's most important to me now."

Candy smiled. She and Crispin stood together and kissed passionately before she explained that she had an hour left in her shift and didn't want to piss off the other girls by just taking off, leaving early, like she'd done before. But she assured him that she would come directly over after work, hopefully to a hot bath and a cup of cocoa.

Crispin's visit to Candy was just the spark she needed to push through the night. Finishing the rest of her shift would be cake now, thanks to a little help from her lover and friend, Crispin. Though Crispin secretly dreaded the impending ritual to make him human, his devotion and commitment to Diana made him smile as he left the club. There would ultimately be a lot to explain to her about the ritual to change him over, but first he'd need to learn a bit more about it himself, so he headed home to read the Cambora and to wait for Di.